Goody's Christmas Wish:

Ebony Goddess Erotic Episodes
Book One

Goody's Christmas Wish:

Ebony Goddess Erotic Episodes
Book One
Written by T'Kendrae M. Ernest

Table of Content

DEDICATION

To my mother, family and friends who inspire, encourage, and challenge me.

THANK YOU

To all the dreamers, visionaries, believers, questioners, and those who possess faith and belief in their hopes and dreams. Thank you for supporting my journey and dream to make my thoughts a real book, not to condemn or judge but to highlight a different and distinct perspective in a world of endless possibilities.

Goody's Christmas Wish:
Ebony Goddess Erotic Episodes
Book One

Goody's Christmas Wish:

Ebony Goddess Erotic Episodes
Book One
Written by T'Kendrae M. Ernest

A letter from the Author:

Good evening everyone reading this. I hope you are reading this in the evening, because I always envisioned the readers of this book to read this series at night and hopefully, through the night, if they weren't doing someone or something else.

Okay, this is an introduction to me and my three-part series of Ebony Goddess Erotic Episodes. The first book features Goody, the Tongue Goddess. I love her. She is such an interesting and complicated character. She is ambitious, standoffish, silly, and bold. In writing about her, I wrote about myself. All the goddesses, in a way, are parts of me and all the women I know and love. They are complicated, caring, fun loving, silly, sensitive, protective individuals, and so much more.

I am writing this letter to introduce myself to the reader of this book and my ambitious three-part series.

The idea of Ebony Goddess Erotic Episodes came to me after reading my umpteenth romance book and being disappointed, finishing it, at the ending. I have to admit that I love romance books, but too often when I read them, I am left unsatisfied. Most romance books I read are all about the chase and little about the capture and passion once the chase ends.

I wanted to read something where the chase is there but wanted the capture and the passion described in vivid detail. I wanted passion and power. I wanted something different. I wanted romance with a lot of kink in it.

I wanted romance that was inexact, awkward, unsure -- like walking into a dark room looking for the light switch. Romance books, at least the ones I read, were fairytales over and over again. The prince, or the princess, would walk into the dark room of an unexpected tryst, an one-night stand, a meeting, and the light switch was always to the left or the right and against the wall. All they had to do was reach for it.

So, I read and read and hoped and wished to find a good and accurate awkward and clumsy and passionate and fumbling romance novel. For me, in my reading, no such luck. Not finding what I wanted, I wrote the Ebony Goddess Erotic Episodes. This is not just romance. This is the chase, the capture, and the passion and pleasure on the other side of the chase. It is a taste of romance and a heavy dose of erotica.

What is the difference between romance and erotica? Well, romance is all about the buildup and detail of the two characters, to me. Again, there is all this build up to the chase and then, finally, the coming together of the hero and the heroine. I like those stories; they are modern day fairytales. The prince and the princess, the cowboy and cowgirl, the tough guy and the rich girl. You get my point? They never, or rarely, detail the two devouring each other. There are a bunch of words that lead to that but not much sexual action in those stories. As a result, I was not satisfied by most romance writing.

Now, on the other hand, erotica usually starts after the meetup and then there are all the awkward looks, glances, and attempts to devour one another and then sex. Don't get the wrong idea, some erotica fails to balance the sex with the story. It is all about sexual gymnastics and sexual positions but for no reason. That is kind of boring.

Now, me. Me? I love sex. I love the passion of it. I love the silliness of it. I especially love the messiness of sex. It is never perfect or what we expect. The first time, the chance encounter that leads to kissing, groping, dry humping and then... everything else is awkward, rough, and rugged, at least, in my experiences.

I am not an expert in sex, by any stretch of the imagination. Never would I suggest that I was. I love sex. I love pleasing my partner. I love my partner pleasing me.

My search for love was never that simple. So, I didn't want to read about an oversimplified love story. I wanted the prince or princess to walk into the dark room and fumble. They could look left or right but the light switch was hanging from a chain in the middle of a cluttered and uncaring room.

It is the fumbling, silly coincidences, and accidental encounters that I didn't see in the romance books I read that were the reason I decided to sit down and write this and the two following books.

So, the difference between this and the following two books is that I am trying to combine the two genres in a less disappointing and boring way. My writing is sexual and romantic, to an extent. You will find in the stories men and women trying to please each other. The men aren't perfect. The women aren't all super models. But they know what they want. Well, the women know what they want. Or seem to have a good idea of what they want. The men, like the women, can be cocksure. At the same time, they can be as confused as anyone. They struggle with what they really want. That might be surprising to some, but some men and women know what it takes to get them where they need to go.

That was my goal. My objective in writing these stories is to make them a little more than modern fairytales or unrealistic romances. Hopefully, after reading this, you will find that the adventures detailed here and elsewhere are more accurate in their inaccuracies, if that is a thing.

This is a book series that is fun, sexy, naughty, lustful and all the time aware of itself. It is about pleasure. It is about losing one part of yourself to discover another part. It is sexual and not some science book. There are some attempts at romance. There are all the things in between kissing and fucking as well. There is the chase and passion in the aftermath. There is definitely a lot of fucking in this and the following books. So be prepared.

The story, Goody's Christmas Wish, is my introduction to you, the reader, to one of the many Ebony Goddesses out there adventuring. This book will be followed up with my second book in the middle of the same year if things align correctly.
Enjoy.

T'Kendrae M. Ernest

Chapter 1.

December 18.

LA was the city of dreams. At least, that is what people say. The Valley, San Fernando Valley, was the city of fucking, sucking, drugs, lights, cameras, and these paper-thin set ups to sex scenes. I learned all that after just seven months in LA. I arrived when I was eighteen. I didn't stick my toe seriously in the industry until I was nineteen and just a few weeks from turning twenty. By the time I was twenty-one I was making my way up through the seedier side of the porn industry and had some dreams and goals.

But before I can get to those things there was a... problem. Jesse. Jesse was not my boyfriend. He was someone I liked. He was, on good days, someone I hung out with, and a good hard dick, but he was not anything more. I know how it sounds, but I was weird about dicks. I didn't let everyone into the gates. I might play around and fondle a hard-on and get all hot and bothered fantasizing about sucking a dick, but I just didn't let just anyone push up in me.

The problem with that was that I let Jesse enter the gates. So, he thought he was my boyfriend. That was a problem. I hated problems.

I was trying to make my life better. I didn't need problems. For a year I worked as a receptionist at an insurance office to pay bills for what seemed forever. In that year I was slowly making my mind up to leave that L-7 job and try and make a clean break of the fake life of working nine-to-five and trying to get into the adult film industry.

I had done some low-grade work and then got the chance to do a higher low-grade film that seemed to get a lot of attention. Somehow, I was making money from the eight videos that were on my ManyFans video channel.

I was low level making a name for myself. People called me and wanted me to audition for things. It was never anything big, but it was getting me noticed. The jobs were never very long, just a few hours in front of the camera, naked, with strangers, cameras, weed, and sometimes drinks.

When I left that I would come back to Jesse. He was a relief. He was friendly and more of a hard dick that I used to get my mind off all the dumb stuff I dealt with. I know it is weird to say that I didn't fuck everyone or that I didn't let everyone in my gates when I was trying to be someone in the industry, but that was how I dealt with all the dicks in my life.

Jesse was my non-business side. I had met him at a house party one of my friends invited me to, almost a year ago. He was handsome. He had big shoulders and a nice smile. On and off for nine months we dipped and dodged each other.

Sometime in August, bored and horny, I ran into Jesse in Westwood. We ended up at my apartment that night.

"I'm not looking for anything long-term," I told him that night.

"I'm good," Jesse said.

So, we kissed. He felt me up. I rubbed his thick chest and let him squeeze my ass. That first night, after Jesse peeled me out of my jeans and I finally got a look at his throbbing pole, we played with each other. We didn't even fuck.

Early that morning though, Jesse woke me with his hard-on. He was spooning me. His hard-on slipped between my thighs, and I guided his hard dick into my longing pussy. The connection was magical. I could not remember the time or the date or if I had locked the front door as Jesse plowed my waking pussy. That pre-dawn fuck was like a dream. Jesse turned me around to spoon him so that he could squeeze my breasts and nibble on my neck. As he kissed my neck, I could feel my body become an open nerve, and I could feel Jesse doing everything all at once. I closed my eyes to heighten the sensations all around me.

While he twisted my nipples and nibbled on my neck, I could feel his cock and balls slapping my ass. All the while that my mind took in that Jesse somehow had freed one of his hands and slipped it to my sensitive clit. I tried to breathe as Jesse found my tingling triangle. He rubbed the lips of my hungry nether mouth.

I loved the feeling of being fingered. That morning, as Jesse rubbed me and plowed me from behind, I closed my eyes to the heady pleasure that washed over me. I liked the overwhelming feeling that came from being touched, kissed, and played with. I wanted to scream but didn't want to scream to make Jesse stop.

Jesse held me in his arms, his free hand rubbing and applying pressure to my clit as his hard dick dug in my guts from behind. I moaned. He pulled his hand from my clit and held me by my hips as his hard dick tried to knock down my wanting pussy walls.

The connection was electric as Jesse pushed his dick deeper into my guts. Jesse pushed his swollen pole farther and as he did, I blindly moaned. The connection, the union, was all that I wanted and nothing else. All I remembered that morning was Jesse riding me from behind and holding my tits and just pounding me until he came and I gave in.

Afterwards, still lying in bed, Jesse and I lay in the afterglow. We didn't talk for a while.

"You good?" Jesse asked.

"I am," I said. "Thank you," I added, letting my hand rest on his chest.

"Cool," Jesse said.

That was how we got together. That was in August. One thing led to another and for the next three months we hooked up and fucked each other's brains out, but that was all. I just wanted a little normal in my life, but nothing more. I tried to tell Jesse that a million times, but he didn't want to hear it. He was sprung. He saw us as something. I didn't. I couldn't.

I didn't want attachments. I had spent most of my adult life avoiding attachments. I had been drawn to the seedier side of the entertainment industry. I was trying to become someone in the adult film industry and could not afford any real attachments.

"These men all get clingy and territorial," Jade said. "They start out thinking that dating and fucking an adult entertainer was like climbing Mount Everest or shooting the winning basket of a championship game. You know?" Jade was a little older than me and trying to be someone. She was sort of my friend in the industry. Jade had taken me under her wing. "Goody, be careful," Jade said. "They start to think that they own us. Then they flip out if we don't call them back. Small things at first, questioning where we were and why we didn't answer their text," Jade said. "We didn't sign up for that."

"But," I said.

"This industry is fucked up. We are all these hard dicks fantasy, but at the same time they want us to be virgins or some shit," Jade said. "We can't win. Once they learn that we are fucking for money things change." Jade paused. "Just be careful. I know too many that end up hurt trying to be something they not."

I didn't need the drama or stress. After a day of entertainment, I just needed someone to cuddle with and nothing more. Of course, everyone I dated I fucked, at least for a while.

Jesse was getting clingy. Thanksgiving, he wanted to meet up. I did not really enjoy the idea of a family gathering. My family was a distant memory. I couldn't remember the last time I had gone to a real Thanksgiving event.

So, I opted out of the Thanksgiving dinner with Jesse. He was not happy with my choice.

All I had was my brains, my body, and my booty. I didn't need attachments. It was sort of my mantra.

So, a week after Thanksgiving he took me to dinner and then back to his apartment. Then, he took me to his bedroom and as we reached his bed, he stopped me.

"Goody," Jesse said after we lay in the afterglow. "I want this to be more. Us to be more."

Fuck, I thought. I wasn't looking for more with Jesse. A weekly fuck was more than enough.

I didn't fuck everybody. I only let a select few in my love shack. It was weird, I know, but I liked blowing guys. It was fun. It was a game to me. I liked seeing how long they could hold out before busting a nut. It never seemed that serious to kiss on some guy's hard dick. But letting someone ride me and break down my walls was reserved and special.

So, letting Jesse dick me and push against my walls was special, in a way. We connected. The fucking connection was sensational. I pushed against his hard cock and every time I did, I grunted with pleasure. I was moaning and grunting like an animal. Jesse held my hips and I pushed back against his hips. The connection was electric. Time fell away and I screamed. The wave of ecstasy washed over me. If only Jesse could have been happy with that.

Instead of dealing with Jesse, I avoided him. All of December I avoided him. He called and texted me, but I did not answer or return the text messages. I know, it was kind of a bitch move. Sue me.

Thankfully, with seven days 'til Christmas I got a call from Phyllis J, AKA Ginger, a long-time friend and stripper from New York.

"Goody? What are you doing for Christmas?" Ginger asked. As soon as she used my alter ego name I knew she was talking party girl business.

"Nothing," I said.

"Well, get your ass to New York. There are three parties that we can go to and make some cash," Ginger said.

"Ginger? What are you talking about?" I asked.

"Girl, you know how you asked me if I had any connections with the big names in the industry? A couple of months ago I upgraded. I was stripping and this promoter says that Porn Mansion is having a pre-Christmas video release. I know the promoter. So, I ask him if he needs any party girls. He says he does and that there's also a movie wrap party from P-Wave the next night he is planning." Ginger shakes her head on camera.

"Wow," I said.

"Fuck ya," Ginger said with a smile. "A couple of days later at the same strip club I meet this guy named: Rudy. Rudy says that there's a big pre-Christmas party with some up-and-coming talent from Hollywood. It is supposed to be the biggest one," she laughed. "So, I got called to wine and dine some big shot New York celebs and they want some fresh faces and party girls. I told my man Todd and Rudy that I knew a down chick from Los Angeles that would be perfect."

"What?" I said, amazed.

"Yeah, girl," Ginger said with a giggle. "I didn't forget about you."

"Thank you, girl, for looking out," I said.

"We got to look out for each other in this cruel world," Ginger said. "We only got us."

"Okay, I'm in," I said. Christmas in New York sounded good.

"Good, I got your hotel room and transportation. You just have to pay for the flight," Ginger said.

"I'll book it after I get off the phone with you," I said. "I'll text you the deets as soon as I book."

December 19.

Life in Los Angeles was nowhere I wanted to be during Christmas. I grew up in Chicago. I had been in Los Angeles for half a decade and every Christmas I missed the snow. So, I figured, with all the Santas in shorts and flipflops and elves wearing bathing suits I should go and see snow and Christmas trees. I booked my flight and prepared to head east.

Now, my flight was thankfully not full as I took off from Los Angeles headed to New York. I was in the air for six hours with a layover in Chicago. I did not mind. I was in no hurry to get to New York. While in the air I thought about my Los Angeles life.

I was twenty-two-years-old and a semi-famous amateur porn star and party girl. In Los Angeles there were several videos of me seen by a million people. I actually had three videos that had one million views. Those videos made me an amateur celebrity of sorts.

There were nearly eight billion people in the world. There were three hundred and thirty million people in the states. I had to believe that at least a dozen people on the plane had seen my throat skills. I was nicknamed: Tongue Goddess. I was filmed tonguing a guy I had just met. I was a voracious dick sucker. The man I tried to suck the soul out of trembled on the video. It was the man, who I could not identify from a line-up, that I made tremble because of my dick teasing that garnered my first million views.

My second video that gained a million views was me slobbing on the hard-on of a semi-professional porn star that had three million followers. I tongued his tip and let him come on my chin and chest. His followers seeing me licking the big black cock and juggling his balls found my small but growing 'Gram channel and ManyFans page and made me an up-and-coming amateur star.

Yet, it was my fifth video, of the hundreds I had of me showing off my tits and ass and the sex videos I had done, that made me an "It" girl and someone people wanted to see up close and personal. I was videoed deep throating a massive penis of another semi-professional porn star who had dated a celebrity for a month in Hollywood. He had six million followers. His followers made me a big unknown. The video highlighted my small waist and shaved pussy. In the same video, the semi-professional porn star drilled me like he was trying to find oil. Before the video ended and the almost porn star shot all over my back, I was so wet and creamy that it looked like my cooch was making whipped cream.

Eight videos had made me one of the popular accounts on ManyFans. My first video was produced by the fourth-tier production company called: Long Dong Productions. Detrick Granger was the producer and director of that video. It was Detrick that introduced me to the semi-pro porn stars.

As the plane bumped along in the sky, I recalled how my life before ManyFans was shit. I had dropped out of school, my senior year when I lived in Chicago. When I turned seventeen, I left home and headed to Los Angeles. I headed to Los Angeles because it was the farthest I could go and still be in the states. Los Angeles seemed to be the exact opposite of Chicago. It was all spread out. There was no real downtown. This was the place where all the stars lived and hung out.

I heard all the stories of people being discovered in Los Angeles. In my head, I figured, why not me? In the back of my mind, when I caught a bus to Los Angeles, I was hoping to run into one of those star makers and hope they would change my life.

Once in Los Angeles, I quickly discovered the two sides of Hollywood. There was the glitz and glamour of Hollywood with the movie premieres, parties, so many parties, for musicians, celebrities, athletes, designers, and so many others. There were all types of celebrities that were being followed by small packs and larger packs of paparazzi.

On the other side there was the dirty side of Hollywood. The dirty side was not in Hollywood proper but in the San Fernando Valley (SFV). The SFV was the home to every manner of porn. There were the top tier porn production companies located in SFV.

There were the second and third-tier porn production companies as well as the fourth and fifth-tier porn houses. The fourth and fifth-tier porn houses were just amateur porn houses that produced really low-level and low-quality videos.

Thankfully, the flight was not crowded, and no one recognized me on the plane ride.

Six hours later my plane landed in Chicago, and I climbed off the commercial plane and made my way to the next gate and next plane. I had a wheelie bag and rolled it behind me looking for my new gate. Men looked at me as I passed but none spoke. I did not expect them to speak. Men liked to look and fantasize.

The two-hour layover was only eighty minutes when I finally sat down in the waiting area. As I sat waiting, dressed in Dr. Marten 1460 boots, black jeans, a college hoody, and leather motorcycle jacket, I noticed a guy smiling at me from two aisles over. Now, if I was anywhere else, I might have thought this guy recognized me.

Wearing oversized sunglasses and a baseball cap was usually enough of a disguise when I left Los Angeles. So, seeing some nobody ogling me from two aisles over was not surprising, but he seemed to be smiling knowingly. Maybe, I thought I was overreacting. Maybe?

I checked my phone and saw that it was just a matter of time before the plane started boarding. While I waited, I texted Ginger to confirm the three parties. I had confirmed before but seeing Mister Nobody looking and smiling at me I needed cover. So, I looked at my phone.

"You are Goody? Goody Wonder? The Tongue Goddess? I can't believe that it is you," Mister Nobody said with a big smile. "I can't believe it's you." He was a peanut headed man in his thirties with a big and friendly smile. He had small eyes, beneath straight eyebrows, and a straight nose. He had short hair and a beer belly, dressed in a holiday sweater, trousers, and cheap leather shoes.

Behind my oversized sunglasses I looked at the man and did not respond. Instead, I looked back to the gate counter and the two agents talking to passengers. I looked at the gate door and saw that it was now open, and another agent was standing there.

"We are boarding our flight to New York by group," the agent said from the opened gate. "Please be sure you check your gate assignment. We will be preboarding anyone who has mobility issues. Then families with children under the age of three."

I climbed to my feet and found the cocksucker fan in front of me. I grabbed my weekender bag and smiled.

"You think I can get a picture with you? Just a quick one?" Mister Nobody asked.

I reluctantly allowed the perv to snap a picture with me with his phone.

"Can I put my arm around you?" Mister Suddenly Annoying asked.

Reluctantly, I nodded.

Mister Annoying wrapped an arm around my shoulder and took another photo.

"Thanks," Mister Nobody said.

I walked to the gate. I handed the gate agent my ticket and boarded.

The flight to New York was uneventful. It was just two hours of me with my headphones on and ignoring the two people in the seats next to me.

When the plane finally landed in New York I was more than relieved. I texted Ginger to tell her I was in the airport.

Before I could call, I received a text.

Please, upon arrival, go to Baggage Claim, there will be a man and car waiting for you. Mister Donovan Scott, promoter.

I looked around as I stepped onto the escalator and headed to baggage claim for the man who was supposed to be waiting for me. At the bottom of the escalator standing near a group of drivers was a white man dressed in a suit with a sign that read: Goody W. in his hand.

I walked to the older white man wearing a dark suit and smiled.

"Are you Miss Goody?" The man asked.

"I am," I said.

"Welcome to New York," the man said with a smile. "I'm Alan. I'm your driver."

I nodded.

"Well, I'm supposed to take a picture and send it to my boss. Then we'll collect your luggage and take you to your hotel," Alan, the driver said.

I nodded. Alan took a picture and sent it to his boss. A minute later, Alan nodded. He smiled. Alan retrieved my luggage from baggage claim, and we headed to the airport parking lot. There sat a black S580 4Matic Mercedes Benz. I climbed in as Ginger texted me.

You landed? They'll be taking you to the hotel. Have fun. Catch up later?

Alan put my luggage in the trunk, and we drove out of the parking lot toward Manhattan.

"You been to New York before?" Alan, the driver, asked as we pulled away from the airport.

I nodded, a little tired after an eight-hour trip. The Mercedes Benz knifed through the late afternoon traffic with the sound of Christmas music playing from the speakers.

I climbed out of the roomy Mercedes after a short ride from the airport and stood in front of the four-star hotel. We were close to Central Park. The Lincoln Center was within walking distance.

In the hotel there were Christmas decorations. The lobby was a red and white striped Christmas fantasy of ornaments, decorations, and statuettes. There was the heady smell of pine and spiced apples, along with the colorful blinking lights and green of the garlands and the three Christmas trees in the lobby. There were several statuettes of elves in green and red attire positioned around the lobby like elves or mini Santas.

Registering was mere function as I was taken to my hotel room by a bellhop who was a small-shouldered man not much older than forty. He had a thick head of hair and looked at me and I immediately knew that the bellhop was someone that recognized me. I smiled at the bellhop and noted that he was not very muscular, but dressed in a white collared long-sleeved shirt, black vest and silver nameplate over his heart that read: Earl. Beneath his name was: Boston.

Earl carrying my two pieces of luggage eyed me as we climbed to the seventh floor. Earl smiled. I tried not to look at Earl the pervert.

At the seventh floor Earl stepped off the elevator and ushered me to my room. The bellhop opened my hotel room. He placed my luggage near the room closet and waited for instruction.

"Thank you," I said. I gave Earl a ten-dollar tip and closed and locked my hotel door after Earl left. I had one full-sized piece of luggage and my weekender for six nights in New York.

I texted Ginger. *Ginger? I'm in.*

I looked out the hotel window and was not surprised to find that there was a small balcony just beyond. I opened the French doors, and the frigid air chilled me from head to toe. I closed the balcony door and shivered. New York in December was definitely colder than Los Angeles.

After a shower I left my hotel room dressed in a thick green turtleneck sweater, red knit scarf, my blue jeans, a pair of Timberlands, red Roots wool mittens, and my motorcycle jacket. On my head was a red Roots wool watch cap. Before leaving the hotel, I stopped at the front desk to ask where the closest diner was located. The receptionist told me of a diner that was just two blocks to the left. It was within walking distance.

I left the hotel and just walking to the sidewalk felt like I had climbed Everest. It was cold on the streets and people were streaming by dressed in suits and puff coats and winter jackets. I thought of turning around but walked the two blocks to the small diner.

The diner was just a dozen tables with a long bar. I sat at an open table and tried to stop shaking. The server appeared. She was a middle-aged woman with thick eyebrows, big eyes and a piggish nose framed by her curly red hair that fell to her shoulders. On her apron was a nameplate that read: Kirsten. Kirsten was wearing a short-sleeved blouse with dark blue trousers and snow boots.

"Hi, sweetie," Kirsten smiled. "You know what you want?"

"Could I have a coffee?" I asked and paused. I looked at Kirsten for a second and exhaled. "I'd like breakfast? Can you make me some scrambled eggs and toast?"

Kirsten smiled and nodded. "Anything else?"

"You got any fruit? Maybe some bacon?" I asked.

"No problem, honey," Kirsten said.

"Thanks," I said, looking down at the menu by my hand.

Kirsten disappeared. I lifted the menu and saw that the diner I was in served breakfast all day. I smiled at the idea. In Los Angeles, as far as I could recall, there was no local diner that served breakfast all day. I looked around the quiet place and noticed that there were maybe ten people in the diner including me.

I ate my breakfast and watched the diner crowd talking, drinking coffee, eating, and staring out the plate glass window.

I paid for my breakfast and headed back to the hotel.

On the way back to the hotel I saw a limousine pull up to the hotel I was heading toward. The limousine idled and a SUV pulled up behind the stretch limousine. Out of the SUV climbed two beefy men in parkas, sunglasses, black trousers, and boots.

I entered the hotel ahead of whoever was in the limousine. I did not pay the commotion any attention as I climbed in the elevator and a man dressed in a business suit walked to the registration desk before the elevator doors closed and took me to the seventh floor.

Ginger texted me around six, while I was lying in bed trying to recover from the long day of travel.

Babygirl, we are going out tonight. Remember we're working three days straight. So, get your ass dressed and meet me at Intercontinental around 10. We'll be in the bar. Glam up.

My first night in New York was supposed to be a low-key recovery, but I wanted to go out. I did not come to New York to sit in my hotel room. So, I glammed up. I took a long shower. I did my hair. I cleaned up.

I perfumed up. My favorite concoction was my personal mix of three delicious fragrances. I had made my own fragrance for years. I dabbled and tinkered. For the New York trip I had created my fruity, sweet, and citrusy fragrance with Caroline Herrera Good Girl Eau de Parfum, Potion Perfume Super Sun, and Ellis Brooklyn Super Fruit Eau de Parfum. I had added a little woodsy tinge to tingle the nose, just a little.

Naked and towel dry, I put in three diamond stud earrings on my right ear, and four on my left. The diamonds were all one-quarter karats, on purpose, to equal two karats of diamonds. I liked the symmetry of the weight of the diamonds in my ears.

I slipped on light blue panties and a matching lace bra. Around my neck I wore a nearly invisible gold chain with a pendant, in diamonds of the two letters of my party girl name. Most called me Goody and thought that was the meaning of the two letters. For me, I leaned toward the idea of Good Witch or Gee Whiz.

On my right wrist I wore my Apple Watch. I liked it as a watch because it could be used as a phone in an emergency. The band and protective covering were white. I liked the contrast to my caramel skin.

I slipped into a slinky black scoop neck dress that accentuated my curves. I had a pair of Fuck Me pumps that were not ho material. They were closed-toed high heels the color of unicorn blood. Depending on the light, they were silver blue or blue green. Around my left ankle I attached a thin anklet.

As I finished dressing, I tried to think what I would wear to fight the cold of the night. I scanned my luggage and found my trench coat. It was not thick, but it was black and fabulous. So, I slipped on my trench coat after calling down for a taxi to take me to the Intercontinental Hotel.

I grabbed my black tiny purse that carried my credit cards, my cell phone, a mini can of mace, lipstick, a tampon, and eyeliner. My purse was a tiny little box designed by one of Los Angeles newest talents. It looked like a case for six cellphones, as it was six inches wide and six inches tall. I liked that it was strongly constructed and was covered in smooth leather and had an adjustable matching leather strap for shoulder carrying.

The trek to the taxi felt like I was taking an ice bath. I shivered for a full minute as I sat in the taxi and the driver looked back waiting for me to tell him where I was going.

"Sorry," I said. "It's cold."

The taxi driver smiled at my comment.

"Can you take me to the Intercontinental Hotel?" I asked.

"Sure thing, lady," the taxi driver said. "It's just on the other side of the park."

The Christmas music of Donny Hathaway played as we drove through the congested streets of New York towards Central Park. The hotel was a five-to-ten-minute walk from my hotel, but I was not walking at night or in the cold.

I climbed out of the taxi and entered the colorfully decorated Intercontinental Hotel. The door attendant opened the door for me as I entered the hotel. I crossed the merrily decorated lobby in white, green, and red, looking for the bar.

In the bar, which was decorated with garlands and lights, I was greeted by Ginger's laugh. She was dressed in a silver dress with matching high heels, next to two men who looked like they were two dogs fighting over a bone. Beside Ginger were two women. One was sipping a drink and dressed in a plum dress. The other woman, short and hippy was wearing a dark blue dress. They studied me as I stopped and watched Ginger stop laughing seeing me in the bar.

"Excuse me," Ginger said to the two men. She pushed away from the bar and nearly tilted and fell in her silver heels as she came running into my arms.

I laughed at the girl who was maybe three or four years my senior. She had curly hair that was pulled back and up in a curly hairdo that looked like a mix between a Mohawk and top knot. From her earlobes hung three strings of gold. Around her throat was a choker with a cameo in the front. Ginger had her nails painted red and white for the holidays. Just visible was her red lace bra.

"Glad you could make it," Ginger said, with a little smile. She hugged me. I hugged her back. "I'm so glad that you made a smart choice and came to Gotham for Christmas." I looked at the bar.

"Ginger, what are you up to?" I asked with a little smile.

"What do you mean?" Ginger said, feigning ignorance. "These guys are harmless. Just some pent-up husbands, looking for some strange."

"Come on," I said.

"Seriously. These cocksuckers are from out of town and looking to have a little fun," Ginger said.

I smiled and looked at the four men at the bar with two women watching Ginger and me.

"Who are they?" I asked.

"Friends of mine. Parisa and Bunny," Ginger smiled. "They're party girls."

"Hmmm," I said.

"We are on our own tonight," Ginger said. "No security. No protection. So, be careful," Ginger added.

I looked around the bar and noted that there were easily twenty people sitting around drinking, talking, and eating bar food. There were easily ten men in the bar, not including the four men circling Ginger and her two friends.

That night Ginger, Parisa, Bunny and I drove around with the four tourists. We hit Level 3, 760, and the Retroclub before the men got handsy.

Ginger was with Alexander, the unofficial leader of the group. Alexander was bearded and big eared. He had a long neck and small shoulders. He did not appear to weigh more than one hundred and sixty pounds. Dressed in a gray suit jacket, long-sleeved collared shirt, and dark trousers, he looked like a math teacher. Ginger played the party girl game perfectly. She was always smiling and laughing at whatever Alexander said. She was a perfect party favor.

Me, on the other hand, I sat bored and listened to Carlos. Carlos told me his life story in the first fifteen minutes of meeting me. They, Alex, Dennis, Jack, and Carlos were high school friends. They had all gone to the same college. They made a pact to become teachers. They, after seven years of teaching, getting married, having children, getting divorced, decided to go to New York for Christmas.

Alexander, Alex, was in a relationship with a woman he was thinking about marrying. Dennis was the flirt of the group. He had gone through a half a dozen girls in two years and was still not ready to settle down. Jack was married a year after Carlos and is still married. He and his wife sometimes needed a little downtime. This trip was Jack's downtime and away time from his wife.

Carlos told me he had gotten married to some woman he had met online and just two years ago divorced. His wife, Marisa, had just stopped participating in the marriage. He gave me too much information.

Before Carlos' data dump I was lukewarm with the round faced, pudgy man dressed in a leather jacket, checked collared shirt, blue jeans, and cheap shoes. I had brushed his crotch, by accident, to check what Carlos was working with. He did not seem to be hiding a monster in his jeans. The conversation alone sunk all interest in the math teacher from Kansas.

Parisa, straight black hair to her shoulders, wearing a plum dress, nuzzled with Jack. The math teacher was not shy to put his hand on Parisa's breasts and ass. Parisa, wide hipped, and small chested, was an exotic beauty. She had cat-like features from her eyes to her nose to her thin and broad mouth.

Bunny, the smallest of the group, standing only five foot tall, was with Dennis, a man a foot taller than Bunny. He was a thin-framed science teacher, who could not have been more than one hundred and seventy pounds wet.

We were in the lounge area of Retroclub and the music was pumping. There was no holiday spirit here. People were on the dance floor shaking what their mama gave 'em. I liked to dance. I liked to just shake and twirl and let the music move me. We danced, Ginger, Parisa, Bunny, and me. Alexander, Jack, Carlos, and Dennis moved around a bit but got bored pretty quickly.

"So, you want to go and do something else?" Jack asked, looking at me and Ginger and the others.

There was always a moment in the night when things took a turn. This was that moment. We had hung with the Kansas teachers and now they were ready to dip their wicks.

I looked at Ginger. She had gotten this party started.

Ginger had Alexander's hands all over her and she was not shy. When I looked at Ginger, she had her hand on Alexander's crotch, checking his package.

"If you want to do something, then how much you thinking?" Ginger asked Alexander.

"How much?" Alexander asked, confused.

"Yeah, baby, nothing is for free," Ginger said.

Alexander frowned. His group frowned as well.

We were in the Retroclub and I climbed to my feet and headed to the exit.

"Where you going?" Carlos asked, grabbing my wrist, suddenly irritated.

"Just going to the bathroom," I said, with a smile, twisting my wrist from his grip.

Ginger seemed unconcerned with the frowns of the looks of the men around her. Parisa seemed a little nervous. Bunny gauged her comfort by Ginger.

Parisa climbed to her feet and followed me toward the exit.

"What the fuck?" Parisa asked.

"Shit happens," I said. "Sometimes you have to know when to get out and run."

"Ginger is my girl and all, but she can't cock tease everyone and not get them upset," Parisa said.

I stopped listening to Parisa. I found the front of the club and there stood two bodybuilder door attendants dressed in leather jackets, gloves, watch caps, jeans, and winter boots.

"Is there a taxi around to take me to my hotel?" I asked.

"Sure babe," one of the bodybuilders said, raising a hand and instantly a taxi pulled up to the front of the club.

"Thanks," I said. I climbed into the back seat of the taxi. Parisa climbed in beside me.

"Where you going?" I asked Parisa.

"I'm heading to Queens," Parisa said.

"Okay, drop me at my hotel," I said to the driver and sat in the taxi as the Christmas music played in the background.

"I'll pay to get me to my hotel. You can pay from there," I said.

At my hotel I climbed out and texted Ginger as I entered the lobby.

You good? Me and Parisa bounced. Not interested in partying with the Kansas math teacher convention.

I headed to my hotel room.

In the elevator Ginger sent me a short video. In the video Ginger was sitting in the familiar setting of the Retroclub. She was jerking off Alexander at the club, where she and Bunny were sitting. Alexander rolled his eyes in his head as he finally dribbled on his jeans.

"Damn, girl," Alexander said, like he had run a mile.

Ginger, in the video, took her hand out of Alexander's jeans and smiled. She made a gesture with her thumb and forefinger dripping with man goo that measured about three inches.

I shook my head.

It was two o'clock when I finally laid down and went to sleep in New York City.

25

Chapter 2.

December 20.

Eastern Standard Time was a bitch. I woke the next day, or the same day I returned to the hotel, in my king-size bed. Christmas music sounded from my phone on the bedside table. I stretched out and found the phone and shut off the alarm. I woke but only in phases. Lying in bed I opened my eyes and looked at the ceiling. My head did not ache. I had drunk a little but nothing too hard. I could hear people moving in the hallway and talking. I rubbed my eyes and sat up. I was dressed in my nightie and panties. It was nearly eleven when I stretched and reached for the TV remote.

I turned on the TV and reached out and picked up the hotel phone. I ordered room service.

Before room service arrived, I cleaned up, just a bit. I grabbed a robe and opened the hotel door for my food. The food was brought in on a cart. The server was a handsome man with dark hair and an athletic build. He was dressed in the uniform of the hotel, long-sleeved collared shirt, black vest, and black trousers. Over his heart was the silver nameplate that read: Jesse. Underneath his name was: Columbus.

I gave Jesse a ten-dollar tip and closed and locked the door behind him as he left. I sat in front of the TV and ate my breakfast. As I ate, I scrolled through the messages I received.

I saw a message from Detrick Granger. He had texted me. The message was short.

GW, if you are interested, I have a TBS job for you. Working 1/9. Three days' work. $3K a day.

I smiled. I giggled at the idea of working for less than $5K. I was semi-famous. I was a semi-professional amateur porn star. I was a legitimate fuck toy on video. I made money sucking dick. I made a lot of money sucking dick. I was the Tongue Goddess. I wanted to be mad at Detrick. I wanted to write him back and tell him that I did not show my tits, give a blowjob or have sex now for less than $10K on video, but I did not. I did not respond.

Instead, I ate my breakfast and hoped for one of the top tier porn producers to respond to my request for an audition.

I texted Ginger after two.

Girl, what did you end up doing? When did you get home?

Ginger called me. We Facetimed.

"Goody, those Kansas boys were marshmallows. They acted like they was going to break us off something," Ginger said, all in the camera. Her hair was all over her head. She looked like she had just woken up. She was wearing a leopard spotted robe and black bra.

Ginger was in her kitchen. In the background were cabinets, a microwave, and stove. Over her right shoulder was a window with blinds. On her kitchen table was a cereal bowl and box of cereal. She had a piece of toast in her hand.

"You didn't fuck them?" I asked.

"Those limp dicks came before we could get that far," Ginger said with a smile.

"What?" I asked, confused.

"Yeah, when you and Parisa disappeared they thought they could double team me and Bunny," Ginger said with a smile. "Bunny horny ass almost blew that science teacher at the club. He kept it together and we all caught a taxicab to Times Square."

"Ginger?" I asked, impatiently.

"Yeah. Yeah," Ginger said. "So, we didn't fuck. They felt on our asses. They felt good at the end of the night."

"Okay," I said, with a shake of my head. I smiled.

"You saw the video?" Ginger asked.

I nodded.

"They were puppies Goody," Ginger said.

"Okay," I said. "So, what is the plan for tonight?"

Ginger gave me the rundown of the pre-Christmas video release from Porn Mansion.

"This is a big baller event," Ginger said. "All the big names are going to be there. Hell, we might even see Montana or Mia or possibly Luscious Lucy roll through."

"I would love to talk to anyone of them about how they got to Porn Mansion," I said to myself "How much?" I asked, curious.

"Todd is giving us $10K for the night," Ginger said on the other end of the phone. "We'll split that."

I knew that the money was not my priority as I wanted to meet some of the movers and shakers who might get me a contract at Porn Mansion. This top tier producer could make my dream of making my own films a reality. I just needed a break.

"FundApp me and I'll be there," I said about to hang up.

"No, that ain't how it works Goody," Ginger said. "We're supposed to come by before five to make sure we're all legit and ready to go. He said that he has to make sure that no girls are clickbait." She paused. "It's his reputation."

I paused and took in the latest information from Ginger.

"Where's the event?" I asked, a little annoyed with the need to be checked out.

"He's set up at an old theater in Midtown where the film will be shown," Ginger said. "I'll text you the address. You can go by any time after two. The cutoff is at five."

I frowned. Just then I got a text message. I looked at the preview of the txt message. I shook my head. It was a text message from Jesse.

"You good?" Ginger asked.

"Yeah. Yeah," I said. I wasn't sure how to deal with Jesse.

"What's up?" Ginger asked, curious.

"It's nothing," I lied. "Just some bullshit back in LA."

"Okay," Ginger said. "Look, Todd don't like you," Ginger said, cautiously. "Then you don't get into the party."

"But I flew out," I said, a little irritated.

"I know," Ginger said. "I got your ass out of LA and here for the audition. That's a no-brainer. You just show up and let him see you are real."

"Casting couch?" I asked, skeptical.

"Maybe," Ginger said. "Be prepared. Todd is a horn dog."

"Okay," I said. "I'll call you later." I hung up with Ginger and found myself trying to weigh the good and bad of being in New York.

It was only two o'clock when Ginger contacted me about the audition with Todd Dougherty. I wanted to meet the heads of Porn Mansion or the producers. So, I could not be mad at Ginger. She was right. I was in New York. All I had to do was go to an audition and let him check me out. No biggie.

In my head, the bigger picture was that this party was a Porn Mansion party. They were a top tier porn production company. They were also in New York to show their range. I liked that and I also knew that whoever was being celebrated, was a big celebrity for Porn Mansion. The company was dedicating their resources to the release of the movie. That was pretty big.

So, I texted Todd.

Hey Todd. Friend of Ginger. Goody from LA. Wanted to come by and let you see that I'm real so I can go to the party. What is a good time? I'm in Manhattan and just a taxi ride away.

I ate lunch and as I was watching TV, Todd Dougherty texted me.

I'm available now. I'll be here until five. Just text when you're on your way.

I got dressed and caught a taxi to Midtown to meet with Todd Dougherty.

The taxi driver stopped and waited for me to exit.

The little theater was in Midtown. It was a typical movie theater artifice with a marquee and lighted sign that set it apart from the storefronts around it.

I walked to the front door and knocked. A man dressed in a three-quarter length leather jacket, gloves, and scarf opened the door and looked at me shivering on the sidewalk.

"Yeah?" The stranger said in a growl.

"I'm here to see Todd Dougherty," I said.

The giant in the leather jacket was wearing sunglasses and a leather Kangol. He nodded and held the door for me to enter.

I was dressed in my Dr. Marten boots, jeans, and my trench coat.

Go back to the stage," the giant said. "He's in an office in the rear of the theater."

I walked through the small lobby and entered the theater proper and took in the intimate 400-seat theater. The theater was a slanted floor that rolled down to a three-foot-high stage. At the stage were half a dozen men and women talking. Two of the men were wearing baseball caps, sweatshirts, jeans, and tool belts. There were two women standing and looking bored. One of the women was wearing a fur coat, oversized sunglasses, and had a Dolly Parton body. She crossed her arms beneath her chest and stood bored. The other girl was more proportional. They both were dressed in jeans, sweaters, and snow boots. Next to them were two men in suits, ties, and listening to one of the men dressed in a dark blue suit with white hair.

"Need this to go off without a hitch, Todd," the man with the white hair said as I arrived.

"I gotcha," Todd said.

The men looked at me. I watched the two women, one blonde, the other ash blonde, watching me. The ash blonde woman with the big tits smiled and pointed at me.

Todd Dougherty was standing with a booted foot on the stage nodding when I stopped in front of the group. He was dressed in leather pants, boots, and a purple and gold silk shirt.

"How can I help you, darling?" The man in leather pants asked with a slight British accent.

"I'm looking for Todd Dougherty," I said, looking at the people onstage. The woman with the fake tits was one of Porn Mansion's bigger sex stars.

"I'm Todd," Todd Dougherty said, extending his hand to me. I shook hands with the promoter. "Perfect timing," Dougherty said. "I got you Charles. We are only here for an hour after the film. Then we head to the ballroom," Dougherty said. "This ain't my first rodeo, mate." He turned and pulled me up and onto the stage. He guided me to the right and backstage. "Come with me," Dougherty said.

We went to his office.

"Thanks for getting me out of that," Dougherty said.

I smiled.

"Okay, before you get all confused," Dougherty said. "I am not connected to Porn Mansion. I just been hired by Porn Mansion as the party planner," the white man with close shaved haircut said. He was a tall, skinny man who ran a dozen clubs in the five boroughs and made a nice chunk of change in his party promoting business. "I'm connected. So, you want in then you go through me." Dougherty was one of those guys that was always looking for an angle. He sized me up and decided to test me.

I waited, knowing that nothing was free.

"Tonight, you are just an after-party girl," Dougherty said. "Be available for pictures. If the people want more that's up to you. I ain't paying you to fuck nobody."

I nodded.

"Now, I heard you are the Tongue Goddess?" Dougherty asked, looking at me.

"I been known to break a man's will," I said.

"Well, can you come over here and show me what I paid for?" the promoter asked with a small smile.

I smiled and nodded.

"You wrap it I'll see what I can do," I said, knowing that in this business nothing was free. There was a cost for everything.

Todd Dougherty smiled. He reached into his desk drawer and pulled out a condom. Dougherty bit the edge of the condom package and opened it. He expertly unzipped his leather pants and rolled the condom onto his stiffening penis.

"You good?" I asked.

Dougherty nodded.

I came to the other side of Dougherty's desk and put my hand on his penis. Dougherty smirked as I massaged the promoter's tiny bit of meat. I did not smile or make any expression. Instead, I massaged Doughtery's bit of manhood and tried to think happy thoughts. I studied his pink index finger long tool. I bent down and got on my knees to be eye-to-eye with Dougherty's one-eyed wienie. I continued to hold Dougherty's pink worm in my hand.

"Come on, bitch, show me that mouth magic," Dougherty said, in a growl.

I licked on the little bit of meat and then sucked on the tip. I let my tongue circle the tip of Dougherty's cock and watched the man in the chair stiffen as my magical mouth unlocked the promoter's dam of passion. In a moment I felt Dougherty stiffen. I did not stop tickling the tip of his dick until I felt Dougherty's leg jerk, just a little, as he released his load into the condom in my mouth.

I looked up and Dougherty closed his eyes. He was one of those types.

Climbing to my feet I looked at Todd Dougherty and smiled.

"Damn, girl, you are amazing," Dougherty said pulling the used condom gingerly off his now limp dick. He made sure not to spill his seed captured in the rubber. Dougherty looked and tossed the condom in the wastebasket by his desk.

"You can go," Dougherty said.

"Any extras for tonight?" I asked, with a smile.

"No," Dougherty said, zipping his pants and trying to regain his composure.

"So, you paying me in cash or bumping my FundApp?" I asked.

"Yeah, I got you," Dougherty said. He pulled out his cellphone and scrolled through the screens. He tapped a few buttons.

I stood waiting. I buttoned my trench coat, opened my purse, and pulled out my cellphone.

"You should be happy," Dougherty said.

I opened my FundApp to see my balance.

"Got it," I said with the bump of cash registered on my FundApp balance.

"You should be at the ballroom," Dougherty said. "The talent should show up between ten and one and you are scheduled to be in that ballroom until two. Don't leave before two."

"Got it," I said. "See you then."

🌲 🌲 🌲 🌲 🌲 🌲

I went back to the hotel. I took a shower and cleaned up just a little and tried not to think of what I had done with Todd Dougherty. I went to get something to eat. I ate in the hotel restaurant and then returned to my room. I texted Ginger to tell her I was good, and I would see her later that night.

I watched a little TV. I took a nap. Then, around eight I began to get ready for my after-party appearance.

I glammed up, like I had the night before. I took a long shower. I did my hair. I cleaned up.

I perfumed up. My favorite concoction was my personal mix of three delicious fragrances. I had made my own fragrance for

32

years. I spritzed my fruity, sweet, and citrusy fragrance on my wrists, between my tits, on my waist and my ankles.

For Porn Mansion I wore my three diamond stud earrings. I opted for black lace panties and a matching bra. Around my neck I wore a thick gold rope necklace.

I changed the band on my Apple Watch. The band and protective covering tonight was gold. I admired the difference to my skin that night.

I slipped into a slinky green V-neck dress that accentuated my curves and rested just a few inches below my round ass.

I wore a pair of gold Fuck Me pumps that were green suede material. They were closed-toed three-inch high heels. Around my left ankle rested a thin golden anklet.

As I finished dressing, I tried to think what I would wear to fight the cold of the night. I grabbed my trench coat. It was not thick, but it was black and fabulous. So, I slipped on my trench coat after calling down for a taxi to take me to the sight of the Porn Mansion after-party.

I grabbed my fashion miracle purse. I loved that it looked like a small gold chained black box. I also liked that it was strongly constructed and was covered in pebbled black leather hide.

I took the elevator to the lobby and crossed the busy space to the exit. Just a few feet from the hotel entrance sat a waiting taxi. I know that it wasn't that far or that cold but dressed as I was the cold chilled me to the core before I climbed into the heated cab.

The taxi driver was a jovial guy named: Jason. His cab was decked out with red and green Christmas lights and as we made our way to Midtown, I listened to Christmas music and felt the season all of a sudden. Jason pulled up to the ballroom, which was in a hotel on the edge of Hell's Kitchen.

I climbed out after paying Jason and giving him a healthy holiday tip and headed into the hotel looking for the ballroom.

Unlike the hotels I had been to earlier, this one had visible security positioned and guarding the entrance to the ballroom. I counted six security guards, big men, watching the entrance. The security guards were all wearing suit jackets, Porn Mansion t-shirts, earpieces, black trousers, comfortable shoes, with a radio on their hip.

At a table next to the only entrance to the ballroom sat people behind a table with a ream of paper in front of each of them. I walked up to the man and smiled.

"I'm Goody Wonder," I said with a smile.

The man, dressed in a suit jacket, collared button front shirt, and a designer watch on his wrist leafed through his stack of papers, looking for my name. The woman, next to the man, was watching me out of the corner of her eye. She looked familiar to me, but as I tried to connect the dots the man found my name and gave me a plastic ID bracelet like in the hospital. Once that plastic bracelet was attached, I knew I would have to cut it off when I finally left the after-party. The bracelet was green. I looked around and noticed that everyone in the lobby of the ballroom had a green plastic ID bracelet.

"Enjoy," the man said with a smile.

The security guard at the door opened the door to the ballroom. I entered to the sound of Eartha Kitt singing Santa Baby. The space was dark and as I entered, I was surprised at the art deco designs and flourishes. The space was a throwback to the 1930's. It was a multi-level space. There was a balcony and catwalk. On the third level of the ballroom was a lounge.

Women in flapper dresses walked around with hors-d'ouevres. Men dressed in gray bowties, white collared button front shirts and gray slacks carried trays with drinks. It was quite the event.

I looked around and saw just about one hundred people milling around the large ballroom that could easily hold ten times that number. I walked around and tried to get a lay of the place. There was a stage at the rear of the ballroom where a DJ was set up to play music.

The center aisle of the ballroom was barren. On either side of the space were fifteen tables. The space was open for dancing, I decided.

"Goody? You made it?" Ginger asked, climbing up from a table with three other women. She was dressed in a spaghetti red and green print dress that showed off her white lace bra. On her head were fabric reindeer antlers. Two of the three I recognized. Parisa and Bunny waved. I smiled at the two and nodded to the unknown woman dressed in a silver front strapless black dress.

The newest member of the party girl crew was Violet. She lived in Hell's Kitchen. Violet said that she was a party girl because she was going to college.

"This pays most of my tuition," Violet said.

By eleven the after-party was in full swing. Ginger, Violet, Parisa, and Bunny dispersed. We were all on the clock. We were supposed to be everywhere all at once. Porn Mansion wanted us available for photos, social media posts, live videos, and whatever else we were comfortable doing.

A little before midnight I tried to go to the second level, the balcony area, out of curiosity, and was stopped by security.

"If you don't have a yellow bracelet, you have to stay on the first floor," the guard said. Behind him stood another security guard watching the stairs and not allowing anyone on the next level.

Returning to the main floor of the ballroom, I mingled with the crowd. I stayed near the stairs that led up to the second floor looking for celebrities.

Ginger appeared.

"We should leave exactly at two," Ginger said.

I agreed. I took a hundred pictures that night if I took one. I pushed away from the stairs to the second floor and walked around the ballroom smiling and looking for porn stars.

On my circuit around the ballroom, I found Rico Steele with his pants down and getting a blowjob from some young blonde actor. I paused and checked out the girl's technique. She was not particularly good, just mechanical, a lot of head movement and more a hand job, but Steele did not seem to care. He rocked back and forth and shoved his dick into the girl's mouth. There were a dozen cameras recording the impromptu head session.

All the while, the blaring music blared and drowned out the sounds of moans and groans.

I pushed away from Rico Steele and the bad weenie whistler knowing that he was a hired cock and in the same boat as I was, except he was male in a dick driven skin industry.

After midnight, things really started happening. The numbers had swollen. There were easily five or six hundred men and women in the main space. I surfed the crowd and stopped any time someone asked me to take a picture. Every picture included a grope of my tits or ass. There were dicks and tits everywhere.

A woman had a crowd around her as she buried her face in another woman's crotch. Again, there were phones out and cameras filming. At a table just a few feet from the two women there was a big chested woman who looked familiar riding on some porn star while sucking off another cock.

Near the bathroom I bumped into Demi Paul and Eva Reid sitting at a table and talking with Moira Stevens and Trudy Hartman. All four had gotten involved with the industry to pay for their college education. Demi and Eva had been in the industry for nearly a decade. The four had been the top stars of Porn Mansion, but time and interest changed.

Ruthie Love, who had been in the industry for nearly a decade, walked up to the five of us and sat down. She was dressed in a V-neck dress that showed off her curves. Even though she had been in the industry for a decade, Jesse looked amazing.

"The industry has changed," Ruthie Love, looking all of forty, said. "I came in and planned on being in it for a couple of years and I planned on banking some money and getting out. The money was good, but it wasn't great. Then things changed. I was offered a different revenue stream. Everyone in this industry needs to diversify."

"Why aren't you running your own company?" Demi asked.

Ruthie Love rubbed her thumb and forefinger together.

"This industry is misogynistic and cruel," Jesse said.

"You ever think of being a producer?" I asked, surprised at Ruthie's response to Demi.

"That sounds easier than it is," Ruthie Love said. "The industry is still dick dominated."

That seemed to be Ruthie Love's answer and she moved onto another question from Trudy Hartman. I listened and after about ten minutes I broke off and continued walking around the ballroom.

As it got closer to one o'clock, I decided to audition for Porn Mansion. There were lots of cameras and photographers. I scanned the crowd and found one of the big names sitting at a table with several of his friends. They were drinking and laughing as I approached. As I drew close to the table one of the porn star's friends raised a chin in my direction.

I knew that the porn star was Panther. He was a well-endowed brother who was known to wreck a woman. So, catching his attention was a bold move by any woman, let alone me.

"What up girl?" One of Panther's friends said and reached out to grab a handful of my ass.

I did not take my eyes off Panther. He looked up from his drink and smiled. He smiled and then and there I figured I would give Porn Mansion something to think about with one of their hottest male talents.

"You want to sit down?" Panther asked.

I nodded and sat at the table with Panther. I pretended to pay attention to the two others at the table, but my focus was on Panther. He was a muscular man with even brown skin, intense dark eyes, a straight nose, and full lips. In his ear was a diamond stud, twice the size of my largest diamond.

He ordered a drink for me.

"What you doing here?" Panther asked, looking me up and down.

"Your real name Panther?" I asked, a little starstruck with the friendliness of Panther.

"No," Panther said with a wolfish smile. "Stage name." He chuckled. "What they call you?"

"Goody?" I said.

"That your real name?" Panther asked with a devilish smile.

I smiled and chuckled, just a little.

"What you into?" Panther asked, looking me over.

"I'm trying to break into the industry," I said with a smile.

We had been at the table for a few minutes when I admitted that.

"You ain't just a party girl?" Panther asked with a wicked grin.

"No," I said. "I got skills."

"Skills?" Panther asked with a smirk. "Show me."

"Here?" I asked.

"Why not. You shy?" Panther asked, with a smile.

"No," I said. I paused. "You got a condom?"

"I'm tested once a week," Panther said. "I can't get on a set without being tested. So, I'm one hundred percent clean."

I hesitated.

"Trust me," Panther said. I hated anyone telling me to trust them. It was a red flag. It was just like someone saying honestly.

"Fine," I said and got my mind on breaking down Panther.

He unzipped his pants, and I laid hands on the man meat of Panther. He was not even hard, and his dick was thick and weighty in my hands. I fished the brown dong from his pants and for half a second admired the girth and beauty of Panther's dick.

"What you going to do?" Panther said as I held his manhood in my hands.

Instantly, I thought how, just that afternoon, I had given a blowjob to a complete stranger to get me into this after-party to give me the chance to blow Panther. I looked at Panther as he smirked, bored suddenly.

I, on the other hand, thought this was my make-or-break moment. This was my time to shine. So, as I prepared to assault his meat. I smiled at what I was hoping to get on camera.

Panther's friends had their phones out and that drew the attention of the photographers in the ballroom. With an audience recording I massaged Panther's manhood and bent down and licked on Panther's meat. Unlike the afternoon blowjob, I took my time. I licked his shaft and worked my tongue around the base of his head. Panther had to have been blown hundreds, if not thousands, of times and been unaffected by mediocre blowjobs. So, I nibbled on his shaft playfully, like a piece of corn. That got a reaction. I nibbled and licked and then returned to kissing the shaft all while holding the base of Panther's hard dick in my hand. Before I could think of anything else, I kissed then sucked on the tip. I let my tongue circle the tip of Panther's cock and watched the porn star at the table finally stiffen as my magical mouth figured out the combination to the porn star's passion. I did not stop tickling the tip of his hard dick with my tongue until Panther's leg jerked, just a little. I pulled Panther's blood engorged dick from my mouth and let him gush into my hand.

I looked up and as Panther came, he closed his eyes. He was one of those types. Most men closed their eyes when they gushed.

At least, most men that I had been with. I was always looking for the one that was different and not like all the others.

"Damn, girl," I heard someone say as I smiled mischievously for the cameras.

"She took his soul," someone in the crowd said as cameras, phones, and people crowded around me and Panther.

A crowd was all around the table. I grabbed a cloth napkin and wiped Panther's jizz from my hand and the front of my dress.

"What's your name?" Someone asked. I climbed to my feet and dropped the soiled napkin on the table and prepared to leave.

"They call me Goody," I said.

Panther's friends called me back to his table. Panther wanted to have lunch. His friends wanted to take me out and drill my brains out. Four other Porn Mansion porn stars asked for my number. I considered a repeat session, but there was no benefit in duplicating my actions.

For thirty minutes before I was supposed to leave the after-party I was a Porn Mansion sensation. I couldn't help but smile at how a blowjob had gotten all that attention. Sadly, those at the party didn't make financial decisions. I needed to find a mover and shaker.

Chapter 3.

December 21.

A little after two o' clock, while the porn stars continued to party, Ginger reminded us that we could leave.

"Let's go to an all-night diner and get something to eat before calling it a night," Ginger said.

Parisa and Bunny were onboard for going to the diner. Violet too was not ready to call it a night. So, we piled into a cab and drove to an all-night diner in Hell's Kitchen.

We sat and ordered coffee. Ginger wanted a piece of cake. Parisa ordered a club sandwich. Bunny ordered a turkey sandwich. Violet asked about the soup. She asked for a BLT sandwich. I ordered a Grilled Cheese sandwich.

"What did you think?" Ginger asked as she ate her German Chocolate cake.

"Hell, girl, it was fun," Bunny said. "I met the Slayer," Bunny said with a wicked smile.

"Is he gay?" Parisa asked, picking at her sandwich.

"Naw," Bunny said. "He just pretty."

Ginger, Violet, and I laughed.

"I saw Moe Cash," Parisa said. "I didn't get to talk to him. He was heading for the lounge."

"Did you see any good dick?" Bunny asked looking at me.

"Well, I caught up with Panther," I said.

The table broke out in laughter. Ginger chuckled. Parisa smiled from ear-to-ear. Bunny shook her head and placed her turkey sandwich back on the plate. Violet put her BLT sandwich down and slapped her hand on the table.

"You rocked Panther's world," Ginger said with a shake of her head.

"You got a mouthful," Parisa said with a smile.

"People talked about it like you had knocked out Mike Tyson or something," Ginger said.

"Shit was crazy," Bunny said with a big smile. She picked up her sandwich and smiled.

"So, what's next?" Ginger asked, looking at me.

"I don't know," I said. I crossed my fingers and shrugged my shoulders.

"You think this is going somewhere?" Violet asked, picking at her sandwich.

I shrugged again. "I can't say." I tried to think if that was how people in this industry were discovered? It seemed pretty fucked up.

"Our girl trying to make a name for herself," Ginger said, proudly. She reached out and placed a hand on my arm.

I smiled.

"Well, I think the highlight of my night was spotting Junior," Parisa said. "I would have sucked him off just like Goody." Everyone at the table shook their head at Parisa's words.

"Pee, you ain't ready for Junior. That boy is horse hung," Bunny said.

"I tried to take a picture with Junior, but too many people were fighting to take his picture," Parisa said. "So, I backed off."

"Shit, this was a good night," Ginger said. "We got paid. The cocksuckers all got pictures of us. My girl broke down Panther on camera. They all know that Todd hooked it up. We'll get some calls from tonight."

"You think so?" Bunny asked.

"Yeah, that is why we do it," Ginger said. "At least, that is why I do it. We trying to fish upstream."

There was a lull in the conversation.

"We all going to be at the P-Wave party tonight?" Ginger asked.

Everyone at the table agreed. We talked for a couple of hours in the little diner with just the server and cashier and us in the diner. The pre-dawn city was still alive. It was quiet, or as quiet as New York City got. In that silence I felt the first pull of sleep. I blinked, fighting off being the first to call it a night.

"I'm heading home," Violet said and fished out her cellphone and called for a cab.

With Violet waiting up and waiting for her cab, I decided my long night was over too. I called for a cab.

Parisa, Bunny, and Ginger said their goodbyes to me and Violet. They returned to eating as Violet and I left the diner and climbed in cabs headed to our respective sleeping spots.

I got back to the hotel at a quarter to five and was asleep by 5:30AM.

I slept until three o'clock.

By four I was eating my first meal. I ordered breakfast from room service. I figured that I deserved it.

While I ate, I scrolled through my messages. While I was eating a waffle, I saw I had a message from Todd Dougherty. In fact, I had a total of seven messages from Dougherty.

I scrolled to the first message and read them in order.

You were a hit at the party. Porn Mansion want to talk with you.

Get back to me. Some people want to talk with you.

Not sure what you did, but you got people talking.

Oh, looks like you knocked the socks off Panther.

There's a video? Wow.

Get back to me. There are some people looking to talk to you.

I'll see you at the P-Wave party tonight.

I finished my breakfast and got dressed. I decided I needed a warmer coat for the last few days in New York. So, I put on my red panties and bra set, my Dr. Martens, jeans, a sweater, scarf, and motorcycle jacket and caught a cab to Times Square.

In the cab ride I called Todd Dougherty.

"Hey, Goody, you seem to have made an impression on some people at the party, last night," Dougherty said.

I listened.

"Well, I have a few people you should get in contact with," Dougherty said.

"Text me their contact info," I said, knowing that it was not that easy.

"Well, here's the thing," Dougherty said, on the other end of the line. "I sort of gave you the opportunity."

"So, if nothing comes from this?" I asked, sitting in the back seat of the cab, making my way to Times Square. "You want what? Two percent of nothing?"

Dougherty laughed, nervously on the other end of the line.

"It's not like that," the promoter said.

"It is," I said. "You ain't my agent. You just got me in the party. Now, P-Wave wants me there too?" I paused. "Send me the contacts. You know that I'm going back to LA in a few days. There's no guarantees that I contact them before I leave New York."

There was a beat. Dougherty was thinking. I am sure he had not expected the conversation to go this way.

"Well, I'll catch up with you tonight at the party," Dougherty said and hung up.

The cab ride ended in Herald Square at the world's largest Macy's Store.

I walked into the mammoth store and took in the watches and jewelry as I tried to find someone to tell me where the coats were. A woman wearing her hair in a tight bun smiled at me as I approached.

"Can you tell me where the coats are?" I asked the woman behind the watches counter.

"They are on the mezzanine," the retail woman said with a smile.

"Thanks," I said and looked around for the escalator. I walked through the crowds and past Gucci and Designer Handbags. As I found the escalator, I saw the Cosmetics and Fragrance department. I mounted the escalator and moved from the first floor to the second floor and Burberry and shoes, before climbing on the escalator to the mezzanine.

Climbing off the escalator I walked around the Cold Weather department, looking for just the right jacket to keep me warm while in New York City. I walked around Macy's for an hour and a half and before I left, I had purchased a faux-fur trim hooded down puffer coat from Ralph Lauren, created for Macy's. I also purchased a pair of knee-high leather boots. My plan was to wear leggings and a short dress and the puffer coat to P-Wave.

I got back to the hotel a little bit before seven o'clock. I had a light lunch of a Caesar's salad, iced tea, and garlic bread in the hotel restaurant. I was working so I did not eat too much. I did not want to bloat.

After eating my meal, I headed to my hotel room.

Ginger texted.

What time are you planning on being at P-Wave?

Eleven.

See you there.

I returned to my room and took a shower. I cleaned up and slipped on a fuck me dress and my new stomp your heart out knee-high boots. My hair was cut into a short Josephine Baker style with a head full of spit black curls with a single curl above my right eyebrow.

Dressed and looking lovely, I called for a cab and around eleven found myself headed to another ballroom, this time in Queens.

It was a chilly night in Queens and when I climbed out of the cab, I found a line of twenty standing near the entrance and trying to get inside and taking pictures of everyone and anyone going in or coming out of the ballroom.

The P-Wave Wrap Party was at a Rooftop Lounge in Queens. I walked up to the line into the club and waved to the security at the door.

"I'm on the list," I said.

"Name?" The man asked.

"Goody Wonder," I said.

The security scanned the list and found my name. He looked at me again and nodded, allowing me to enter.

The P-Wave Wrap party was the exact opposite of the Porn Mansion party the night before. The party was intimate and on the third floor of the ballroom. In the small lounge that could hold three hundred there was a DJ positioned in the corner of the space against a window that looked out over the snow-covered streets below.

There was a twenty-seven-foot-long bar resting against the rear of the lounge. There were two bartenders dressed in white collared shirts with black bowties and black aprons. One of the bartenders was a bald man with a nose ring. The other was a round faced woman with dreadlocks and finger tattoos. She had a nose ring as well.

As I scanned the crowd, I saw Parisa and then Ginger. The two moved toward me. Out of the corner of my eye I saw movement and there was Todd Doherty. He was dressed in a long black trench coat, a yellow silk shirt, gold rope chain around his neck, and his leather pants and boots.

"Glad you could make it," Dougherty said with a big smile. His smile did not seem friendly, I thought.

I frowned. I gave this guy a blowjob, I thought, and he is acting all weird with me in some club in Queens. The fuck?

"Hi," I said with my fakest smile.

"You got a few heads looking at talking to you," Dougherty said.

"Good," I said. "Give me their numbers or not." I smiled. "I know how to get in contact with them. It will just take a little longer if I have to figure it out."

Dougherty looked at me and frowned.

"You know I'm going to tell them you didn't want to let me talk to them because you were being petty," I said, with a smile as people talked, walked, and sipped on cocktails around us.

Ginger and Parisa arrived and looked at me and Dougherty smiling at each other.

"You two look adorable," Ginger said with a laugh.

"I'll text you," said Dougherty as he walked into the crowd.

"So, what gives?" Parisa asked, looking at me and then the retreating Dougherty.

"Nothing, girl," I said. "Just putting a dog in place."

Parisa and Ginger looked at me, confused.

"Don't trip," I said. "What are we expected to do, tonight?"

"This is just a meet and greet," Ginger said. "We just mingle. P-Wave just likes a bunch of pretty people at their events. Nothing more. No freaky activities, as far as I know."

"We here until, when?" I asked.

"I guess the regular," Ginger said.

I nodded.

So, for the next couple of hours I walked around the lounge and smiled. I took pictures with random guys and girls. I was a living party favor.

True to his word, Dougherty texted me and sent me three text messages. Two of the messages were from Porn Mansion. The third was from Dougherty.

You are definitely the real deal, Goody. Respect. T.D.

I smiled at the message. I was not sure what Dougherty was referring to, but at the same time, I did not care. I had what I wanted.

The worst part of dealing with someone like Dougherty was that for the two messages he sent he was probably withholding two more.

I did not let Dougherty get in my head. That night I danced with some of the P-Wave talent. There was Baptiste, a handsome dark-skinned man who looked like he could have been a bodybuilder. He looked like he was living and breathing chocolate and had a scent of cocoa on his skin. I also danced with Parker

I danced with Rosa Sinclair, one of P-Wave's hottest porn stars, and her on again and off again love interest, Jules Harding.

"You are Goody? From last night?" Rosa Sinclair said after we danced. We were standing at one of the two dozen small round tables positioned around the lounge. Jules Harding was drinking champagne.

"I am," I said.

"You caused a lot of talk," Rosa Sinclair said. "Panther talked about you for a long time after you broke him down."

I did not know that. I nodded, pretending to care. I studied Rosa Sinclair and her compact body. She was dressed in a white sequined dress. Jules Harding was wearing a tuxedo jacket with an opened button front shirt and tuxedo pants. They were the stars of the recent P-Wave movie that was filmed in New York City.

P-Wave was trying to do longer form skin flicks for some reason. There was a rumor that the company was moving to softer porn in an effort to become more legitimate to their investors. I was not putting my hopes in P-Wave. I was putting my hopes in myself.

Chapter 4.

December 22.

At two o'clock we left the P-Wave party. Ginger and the other girls went to a diner in Queens. I chose to go back to the hotel. The night was young, relatively, and it was cold. I caught a cab back to the hotel.

It was just three days 'til Christmas, I thought as I entered the hotel and was greeted by the red and white striped decorations and green of the garlands and the three Christmas trees in the lobby.

When I got back to the hotel room, I still was not sleepy.

I sat in the hotel room and tried to think who I might call. It was just midnight in California. It was two o'clock in Chicago.

All my friends in Los Angeles would be out and partying and I did not want to call them and hear them telling me they were out and partying. Of course, I thought about Jesse. That man was a dead end, sadly. He wanted more than I was willing to give.

I thought about all the people in Chicago that I could call. The list was short. I had not talked to my mom in years. My dad was dead. My older brother was MIA since I was in high school.

I decided to go to the hotel bar and see who was still up. The hotel bar was a small ten-foot by ten-foot bar with a dozen tables and a small stage in the rear of the space. I entered the place and found half a dozen people sitting at tables and just three people at the bar. I sat at the far end of the bar, closest to the stage.

The stage, more an elevated platform, looked like it was set up for karaoke. There was a microphone stand, minus a microphone, two speakers, a video monitor, and some equipment under a black piece of fabric.

"What can I get you?" the bartender asked. He was a short-haired man with small dark eyes, a sharp nose, and thin-lipped mouth. He was dressed in a white long-sleeved shirt with rolled up sleeves that displayed his dozen visible tattoos. The bartender was thin and tall, maybe six-feet-tall.

"You still serving drinks?" I asked.

"Yep," the bartender said. "We serve 'til three." He added, "The kitchen is closed here. If you want food, you have to order room service."

"What is the bar special?" I asked.

"Well," the bartender said, thinking. "Have you tried the Vampiro? Or the Agave Kiss?"

"Never tried either," I said, thinking that I needed to be adventurous in New York. "I'll try the Agave Kiss."

"Coming right up," the bartender said. He went to mix the drink. I watched as he grabbed a pre-chilled lowball glass. He moistened the glass with Chambord then rolled some white chocolate flakes on the rim. He poured in a little Double Cream, a little Crème De Cacao White and topped it off with Tequila Silver in a shaker with ice. The bartender shook the ingredients in the shaker and strained the mixture into the waiting lowball glass. He garnished the drink with a slice of strawberry.

"Enjoy," the bartender said.

"That looks very holiday special," a man sitting at the bar said. I looked up and saw that the man sitting at the bar was dressed in blue suit jacket and trousers. On his feet were some very polished black buckle leather shoes. He was wearing a light blue button front collared shirt without a tie and unbuttoned at the throat.

The man was the color of milk chocolate with dark features, a strong jaw and easy smile. His hair was cut into a tight fade. He did not have any jewelry on. I checked to see if he had a wedding ring.

I smiled at the man's comments. Just then I received a text from Ginger.

The party tomorrow is going to be bigger than PM. This is a celebrity birthday party. Can you believe it? Think it's a movie star. I'll text you deets as soon as I get them.

I smiled and drank my Agave Kiss. I was surprised at how good the drink tasted. It was suddenly my new cocktail. I smiled at the bartender and nodded to him for the liquid creation.

I sipped my drink and casually looked around the bar to see who the people were sitting in the hotel bar at nearly three in the morning. The guy who talked to me was good looking but there had to be some flaw. He was there alone. Three in the morning dressed like he was getting off work as a banker, but that did not make sense. No banks were open this late. So, red flag.

Looking around the three tables, where there were people, I kind of figured the others out. The others, in my mind, in the bar were paired up and trying to screw up the courage to end the night in bed. Some were hoping to get lucky. Some were just heading to bed.

I drank my cocktail and after I finished, I just listened to some music. I started to feel tired and after fifteen minutes I paid my bill. I thanked the bartender and left the bar. I headed to the elevator.

Before I reached the elevator the guy from the bar was on my trail. I turned and stopped. He stopped as well, like a kid caught with his hand in the cookie jar.

"I don't know what you are thinking in that head of yours," I said. "I don't care. All I can tell you is that I will not be involved in it in anyway."

The man smiled. "Well, is it against the law to share an elevator?"

"At three o'clock in the morning, it sure in the hell is," I said. I turned and walked directly to the lobby and registration desk. At the registration desk I looked back and the man did not move from his spot. He just loitered by the elevator.

"I need security to escort me to my room," I said to the receptionist. The receptionist nodded. A few minutes later a security guard arrived at the receptionist desk.

"This is Spencer," the receptionist said. "He'll escort you to your room."

"Thanks," I said.

Spencer was a brawny man, six-foot-two and two hundred and twenty pounds, at least, dressed in a gray suit jacket and gray trousers. He had a white button front shirt with an earpiece in his left ear and a radio under his jacket. He looked like he could have been a linebacker for a professional football team.

"Where you going?" Spencer asked.

I told him all he needed to know. Spencer nodded and looked around the lobby for the man. He was nowhere to be seen. We walked to the elevator and the man from the bar seeing the security guard walked to the elevator and pressed the button for the elevator. The three of us waited for the elevator. I stood with Spencer in between us.

When the elevator arrived, I reached out and whispered to Spencer. The security guard let the man climb on the elevator and then Spencer and I stepped on the elevator.

"What floor are you going to, sir?" Spencer asked.

"Five," the man said. Spencer pressed five. He did not press any other floor.

The lift rose to the fifth floor. The man stepped off the elevator.

The elevator doors closed.

"We'll press seven, eight, and nine," Spencer said. "That should throw him off. If he bothers you, just call down to reception. We don't tolerate any harassment of guests."

"Thanks," I said.

We climbed off the elevator to my floor. Spencer walked me to my hotel room. I gave Spencer a ten-dollar tip and locked the door behind me.

I laid in bed and listened for any strange noises. Hearing nothing I fell asleep around four o'clock.

🌲 🌲 🌲 🌲 🌲 🌲

A little before noon I woke up. I turned on the TV and tried to clear my head. After about twenty minutes I got out of bed and went to take a shower.

After my shower I called the two numbers Dougherty had given me. The first number was for some guy named: Marseille.

"Hi, this is Marseille Cross, head of talent for Porn Mansion, the largest distributor of adult entertainment. Leave a message after the tone. I'll get back to you as soon as I can," his message said.

I left a short message and my number.

The second number I called was for a guy named: James Rokker.

"Hello," said Rokker.

"Hello," I said.

"Who is this?"

"I'm Goody Wonder," I said, surprised that I had a direct phone number to someone at Porn Mansion. "I'm sorry. I got your number from the promoter. I was at the party two nights ago."

"Refresh my memory," Rokker said.

"I was the girl that gave Panther the best head in his life," I said.

"Oh," Rokker said on the other end of the call.

"So, I was told to call you," I said.

"Right. Right," Rokker said. He paused. "You don't live in New York? Do you?"

"No," I said. "I live in LA."

"Okay," Rokker said, measured. "We are interested in fresh faces and new talent. When you get back to California, give me a call and we'll set up an audition." He paused. "I'm sorry that I don't have time to try and meet with you while you are here, but we came out for the video release and now we're heading back to LA tomorrow."

"I understand," I said.

"How old are you?" Rokker asked.

"I'm 22," I said.

"Okay, I have your number and you have mine," Rokker said. "Give me a call when you get back in LA. We're shut down for the holidays and won't be back in the offices until after the fourth."

"Okay," I said, with a smile spreading across my face.

"I'll expect you to call," Rokker said. "Don't forget."

"I won't," I said. "And thanks."

He rung off. I sat on my bed trying to think what had just happened. I had an audition with one of the largest distributors of adult entertainment when I returned to LA. Fuck.

By two o'clock I got a text from Ginger.

We are meeting up in Staten Island. Here's the address. Be there by ten. Ask for Donovan Scott.

I cleaned up and slipped on a fuck me dress and stomp your heart out heels. My hair was a sea of black curls pressed to my head usually with a single curl dancing precariously above my right eyebrow.

A little after ten o'clock I found myself at a roller-skating rink on Staten Island. The rink was pretty popular, but it was a few days before Christmas and there were not too many cars parked in the lot when the Uber driver pulled up to drop me off.

The parking lot had thinned out as the rink had closed at ten o'clock to all regular customers. There was a private party scheduled. A tour bus was idling beside the front of the skating rink. There were three Maybachs parked just a stone's throw from the entrance. As I arrived a Lamborghini pulled up behind a Ferrari and Porsche Cayenne.

Whoever the celebrity was there was a bunch of money invited to celebrate the birthday, I deduced.

"Who rented this place?" the Uber driver asked.

"I'm not sure," I said to the Uber driver, who had driven me from Manhattan to Staten Island. I climbed out of the Uber and braced myself for the cold. Dressed in my newly purchased coat and knee-high boots, I walked to the entrance of the skating rink.

There were two security guards at the front doors of the rink.

I walked up to the men and told them I was invited.

"I was invited by Donovan Scott," I said.

The security were standing in the small alcove of the entry that allowed them protection from the cold. One had a computer with a list of guests. The other had a paper list.

"Name?" The block of stone masquerading as a security guard asked.

"Goody," I said. "Goody Wonder," I said with a slight smile.

Both men scanned their lists and the one with the computer found my name first.

"She's good," the man announced. That stopped the second man from searching.

The whole verification took two minutes.

I entered the skating rink. I had seen movies about old skating rinks, and this was a throwback to the times when people came to these places. I walked through a small lobby with a multi-colored carpet. There were pictures behind a glass, like this place was an old-fashioned high school. Behind the glass were pictures of the life of the skating rink. There were black and white pictures, hundreds of them from the seventies. There were Polaroids and snapshots that captured the eighties. There were pictures from the nineties and into the two thousands.

Just based on the pictures the rink had been around for at least four decades. I smiled at the longevity of a place like this. There was a loyal group that kept the rink going.

I walked around a hallway and to the main area of the skating rink with the sound of the O'Jays singing. The rink was just a big space with a black railing wrapped in red and green ribbons that separated the rink from the lighted and festive seating area, arcade, bar, and rental area. The rental area was the biggest space not the rink. It sat in the middle of the space with a thirty-foot garland draped along its length. I took in the display case that showed off the trophies and awards the place had received through the years.

On the far side of the rental area was a wall and then a bathroom, then another wall. On the other side of the wall was the arcade, lockers, and the bar. On the opposite side of the rental was another wall and a locked door that had a sign on it.

In the area closest to the rink and adjacent to the bar was the DJ booth. The booth was just an open window to look out onto the rink and the seating area. Inside the booth I watched as a bearded and big bellied man wearing a sweatshirt and a pair of headphones mixed music as maybe twenty or thirty people skated in circles on the rink to the sound of the familiar, throaty Eartha Kitt.

The music was surprisingly festive. It was a mix of holiday music, but mostly classic and R&B. As I tried to figure out who was who disco lights flashed in multi-colors as Boys II Men began singing. On the railing were the familiar faces of Ginger, Parisa and Bunny.

Ginger was dressed in a white dress that was trimmed in lace and fell just above her knees. Parisa was dressed in a green and yellow dress that showed off her curves. Bunny was dressed in a green dress that rested a few inches off her round ass with fishnet stockings.

Still bundled up and trying to shake off the coldness of the air I walked to the girls.

Bunny smiled and waved as I approached. Ginger and Parisa turned and smiled, holding onto the railing. Getting closer I almost bust out laughing.

"You are kidding me?" I asked, seeing that all three were wearing white rental skates.

"What?" Ginger asked.

"You don't skate?" Bubble asked, looking at me confused.

I shook my head in answer.

"Girl, it is fun," Parisa said.

"Get you some skates," Ginger said, clutching the railing.

I chuckled at the idea.

Just then a group of six men flashed by on roller skates. Several of them were wearing elf and Santa hats and laughing. They were talking and skating like it was nothing.

Behind the men were a dozen women. Some were dressed in jeans. Some were in dresses. Others in skirts. In pairs and groups of three and four more people flashed by making their way around the rink.

"You need to try," Bunny said. On her feet were white roller skates. "It ain't that hard."

"The floor looks pretty hard to me," I said, looking at the wooden floor.

Several more people skated past as Parisa and Bunny pushed off the railing and onto the rink floor. Ginger smiled and pushed off the railing.

I walked to the rental area and checked my coat. While I was there, I spoke to one of the counter workers.

"What's all of this about?" I asked. "I mean, who's birthday is it?"

The counter worker looked at me and then over my shoulder. He pointed and I turned and followed the arm and pointing finger.

Just coming off the rink was Jamal Jameison, dressed in a Santa hat, green holiday sweater, jeans, and roller skates. I did a double take.

Jamal Jameison was this dark chocolate treat. He was ruggedly handsome with piercing eyes, a straight round nose, luscious lips, and a bewitching smile. Jamal Jameison was not just a pretty boy. He was a tough kid. He had started his life in a tough West Oakland neighborhood in California. He had survived and thrived against all odds and played basketball and football and graduated from high school. Against all odds he had gotten a scholarship to one of the most prestigious schools in the nation and while there did a little acting. Once he graduated, Jamal decided to go to college on the east coast and study acting. It was a bold move, but it paid off. On the east coast he got a chance to do plays in New York. While doing a play he was offered a small role in a film. His presence in his first film spring boarded him to other films. In just five years, Jamal Jameison was in some of the biggest films. He even had action figures made of him.

Jamal Jameison had acted with A-list actors and actresses. He had won an Emmy and been in a Netflix series. I tried to remember what I saw about Jamal Jameison last. He was in New York doing a play.

Jamal Jameison had been linked to one of the NBA player's ex-wives. That alone got him a million followers. He was important in the black community and the acting community. He had over two million followers on every social media platform. I was a bit of a Jamal Jameison fan.

I stood at the counter and watched as casually as possible as Jamal Jameison and his entourage of friends sat down near the edge of the rink, near the DJ booth.

People walked across the carpet and climbed onto the wooden floor to skate. There were easily sixty or so people at the rink. There were easily a 2:1 ratio of women to men. As I scanned the corner, I noticed that there were a handful of kids skating on the rink.

I leaned on the counter and watched as Jamal Jameison sat laughing and talking with his friends. Behind Jamal were a group of women trying to catch the attention of the movie star.

Feeling a little stalkerish I pushed away from the counter and walked back to the seating area where Parisa and Bunny were seated. For a brief moment I considered camping out with the other Looky Lous.

"You didn't get skates?" Bunny asked seeing me approach.

I shook my head.

"I think I'm going to the bar," I said. "Anyone want anything?"

Parisa shook her head. Bunny shook her head and walked toward the rink.

I walked to the bar. The bar was open and the drinks free. There were a dozen people in the bar when I arrived. The bar was near Jamal Jameison and while I waited I watched him sitting and talking with his friends.

With an Agave Kiss in hand, my newest favorite drink, I walked back to the seating area where Parisa and Violet were sitting.

"When did you get here?" I asked Violet.

"About ten minutes ago," Violet said.

"Did you see who is here?" I asked.

Violet nodded.

"Sort of a big deal," Parisa said.

"Yeah," I said, trying not to sound like a groupie.

"So, we just here to be available for pictures," Violet asked.

No one spoke. No one seemed to have an answer. Just then Ginger and Bunny stepped off the rink. The two made their way to us.

"Ginger seems to know everything," Parisa said.

Ginger and Bunny rolled and walked to our little group. The two sat down. Ginger smiled.

"You know you got to get out on the rink?" Ginger said to me.

I shook my head. Parisa smiled. Violet, dressed in a purple dress and high heels, chuckled.

"Ginger? We trying to figure out what's the deal tonight," Violet said.

"Well, we have to find Donovan Scott," Ginger said, getting serious.

"You know who he is?" Violet asked.

Ginger shook her head, looking and smiling at a man passing by. "I have been trying to find Donovan Scott, but so far no luck," Ginger said.

"Wonder if he's out there skating with Jamal Jameison," I said, trying to sound casual.

A few minutes later, Jamal Jameison stepped off the rink and made his way to the corner just below where the DJ's booth sat.

In that corner of the rink, two security guards dressed in heavy leather jackets sat watching everyone.

"So, Ginger, you go and talk to the entourage and see if Donovan Scott is there," Violet said. Paris and Bunny agreed.

Ginger frowned.

"I'll go with you," I said. "You don't want to go alone," I said as casually as possible.

"Fine," Ginger said. She climbed to her feet. I walked with Ginger to the far side of the rink. One of the security guards stood up and stopped our approach.

"Yes?" The brute dressed in a leather jacket which seemed to begin at his ears and fell to his waist.

"I'm looking for Donovan Scott," Ginger said. I stood next to Ginger and peered around the security guard stopping us from getting close to the six men sitting and talking. Some of the men were wearing long-sleeved shirts and gold chains. Some were wearing silk shirts and flashy watches. One of the men close to Jamal Jameison was still wearing his green holiday sweater with a black polo shirt underneath, black jeans, and black roller skates. He had a black Apple watch on his wrist. Of the crowd of people, he seemed the oddest.

The second security guard walked to the group and said something. The man in the black polo shirt climbed to his feet. He fished out his cellphone. As the unknown man reached the security he paused.

"Hi," the man said with a smile. "I'm Donovan. Donovan Scott."

"Hey, Donovan," Ginger said with a smile. "I been texting you. We just need to know what you want from us."

Donovan Scott nodded. He smiled and walked away from security and toward the bar. He stopped at the step to the bar.

"Today is Jamal's birthday. He wanted to have a little fun. This is a long night for us. Jamal isn't going to be here for that long. He just wants some company. Nothing crazy. Just company."

Ginger and I listened to the longtime friend of Jamal Jameison.

"Nothing freaky," Donovan said. "This is just a low-key event for my boy."

"So, do we get to hang out with Jamal?" I asked, trying to be calm and casual.

"Yeah," Donovan Scott said. "Of course," he smiled and nodded.

I wanted to scream.

Chapter 5.

December 23.

Jamal Jameison was funny. He was silly. He had a twisted sense of humor. It took a couple of hours to see that side of the celebrity.

The entourage of Jameison's close friends included his manager, Wild Bill Porter, his personal assistant, Cody Garland, his agent, Lawrence Flowers, the super promoter, Donovan Scott, his personal lawyer, Oscar Younger, and his partner in his new production company, J2 Production, Jason Terry. Jamal Jameison had grown up with most of them. Well, a few of them. Most of them he knew from school.

I learned all this an hour before Jamal Jameison decided to leave the skating rink and get something to eat. The party was ending, and Jamal Jameison and his entourage were hungry.

"We're heading back to Manhattan," Donovan Scott said. "You can come with if you want."

Of course, I was going. I was saddened that I did not get to ride with Jamal Jameison. I was in a Mercedes-Maybach S580 4Matic with Wild Bill Porter, Lawrence Flowers, and Donovan Scott. The car was being driven by Jason Terry.

"So, I heard that you are a throat goat," Wild Bill Porter asked from the front of the luxurious Maybach.

Ginger was sitting in the black Maybach with me. No girls climbed into a car alone. She smiled. She looked at me and licked her lips.

"I'm not the throat goat, but I don't disappoint," Ginger said. Lawrence Flowers smiled at Ginger. He edged closer to her and placed an arm around her shoulder. Ginger leaned in and placed a hand on Flowers' chest.

"If you wrap it, I'll see if I can make you happy," Ginger said.

Donovan Scott, sitting in the back of the Maybach next to me and Ginger smiled. He looked at me with a little devilish smile.

"Thought you said, 'Nothing freaky'," I said with a smile.

"It ain't nothing freaky about some freaky consenting adults," Donovan Scott said. He produced a condom and smiled bigger. "You got to pay to play," Donovan Scott said.

So, Ginger and I gave Lawrence Flowers and Donovan Scott blowjobs in the back of a $200,000 dollar luxury car. I watched Ginger pistoning up and down on Flowers' hard-on in the back seat. I watched and licked on Donovan Scott's stiff dick like a popsicle excited watching Ginger. I watched as Ginger sucked and sucked until Porter's arms stiffened and he shot a load into his condom. Ginger sat up and playfully tapped Porter's limp flesh.

Simultaneously, as Ginger drained Porter's trembling pipe for the moment, I worked Scott. I did not give him my best. I tongued Scott's shaft and felt him stiffen, just a little. I simply held his shaft and sucked on his tip until the promoter surrendered to my practiced fellatio.

"Damn, they that good?" Porter said, with a wicked smile.

"They good," Flowers said, regaining his composure and slipping his flaccid dick back in his pants.

The two Maybachs double parked on the street just outside of a 24-Hour eatery.

"Wait a minute," Terry said, as Lawrence Flowers opened the car door. "Me and Wild Bill need a little taste of your talents before we go inside."

"Yeah, remember I'm Jamal's manager. If you want to play you got to pay," Wild Bill Porter said.

As soon as Porter said those words, I focused on him. I looked at Ginger and raised my chin toward Wild Bill. Ginger only smiled.

Donovan Scott climbed out of the Maybach and he and Flowers walked into the diner.

Terry double parked the Maybach and climbed into the back seat with Ginger and me. Wild Bill followed, opening the passenger door closest to me.

Once in the back seat Terry produced a condom. Wild Bill sat and handed me a condom. I smiled and hoped that my magic would spread to Jamal Jameison. Stranger things had happened, in my life.

I thought how getting to New York was just a string of unrelated things that found me backstage at some Brooklyn theater giving a skivvy promoter a blowjob and that had led me to helping the manager of one of the hottest under thirty actors put on a condom. Being the Tongue Goddess had its benefits. I looked at Wild Bill Porter and smiled.

I planned on hitting him with my regular routine. It was important to impress but not cripple the man. I wanted him to be ready to tell Jamal Jameison I was someone he should fuck with. So, I tickled Wild Bill Porter's erection. The manager was one of those guys that enjoyed sex but thought he could control it if he did not get too excited. I knew the type. So, I played with him and tried to break his will, but not too quickly.

Blowing a guy, to me, was seeing him get into it. That was the carrot, so to speak, for me when I looked at the guy writhing and squirming with pleasure. Now, with Ginger just a few feet away, in the back seat, I got to see her gobbling down the dick of someone and pleasing him. It made me excited more so than when I just watched a guy enjoying me breaking down his walls.

So, I looked at Wild Bill Porter and watched him as he seemed to try to think of something else. That whole mind over matter thing did not work with me as I worked him from stem to stern, looking for the key to unlocking the controls of Porter's milkshake maker. I reached up and rubbed Porter's stomach and that slight touch was enough to have Porter gush a milkshake into the plastic container.

Ginger and I walked into the 24-Hour diner and sat down next to Donovan Scott. A few minutes later, in walked Parisa, Bunny and Violet. They looked as if they had been initiated by Cody and Oscar Younger and two other men, I did not recognize from the skating rink.

The last to arrive were Jamal Jameison and his personal bodyguard, Seneca. Seneca was a thickly muscular individual that looked like he should be a professional wrestler rather than a bodyguard. Jameison came in the diner and sat at the table with me, Ginger, Lawrence Flowers, and Donovan Scott.

"Okay," Jamal Jameison said, after we all took pictures with the A-lister. The entire group had ordered. Jamal studied us with a big smile. He was looking at me and Ginger. "I heard you two are a couple of naughty girls."

Ginger looked at me and I looked at her. Ginger smiled mischievously. I looked directly at Jamal Jameison and imagined being nasty with the A-list actor.

"My boys are saying that you are Throat Goats," Jameison said with a laugh. "I had to tell them that the Goat title is given to just about anyone. That takes away from a real Goat."

"These girls are incredible," Flowers said.

"Well," Donovan Scott said with a smile. "Goody is amazing."

"I can vouch for Ginger," Porter said.

Ginger smiled.

Jamal Jameison shook his head at Wild Bill's comments.

"I don't really care about that," the movie star said, sitting at the diner table dressed in a black polo shirt and leather motorcycle jacket. On his wrist was an expensive wristwatch. "I know that everyone has a hustle. I ain't judging, but what's your deal? Are you hos?"

"What? No, we ain't hos," Ginger said, angry.

"What the fuck?" Parisa said, annoyed and insulted.

"I didn't mean anything by that," Jamal Jameison said with a smile. "I mean, what's your plan? You can't be party girls forever."

I opened my mouth only to close it.

"We can be party girls as long as we want," Ginger said, defensively. "Then we can be Milfs and Gilfs and Cougars if we want," Ginger said. "It's so crazy that when it comes to women owning their sexuality there's all these concerns."

"Double standards," Bunny said from the adjacent table.

Jameison shook his head. "I didn't mean anything by it," Jameison said. "I just grew up around women that thought they could get somewhere on their backs." He paused. "That didn't happen."

"There aren't a bunch of choices for us," I said. "We have to work with what we're given."

Jamal Jameison smiled. "We all do," Jameison said.

We ordered our food. Jameison ordered eggs, turkey sausage, and waffles. Ginger ordered a cheeseburger and fries with a

Coke. Flowers ordered a turkey sandwich and a soda, Scott ordered a burger and fries with a milkshake, and I ordered eggs and waffles, like Jameison.

Jameison sat and studied all the people in the diner. "You know that I have been to a lot of places. Been to some amazing places. New York is unique. Other cities try to imitate it but it's not the same." He paused. "I mean, where else you going to find something like this?" He brightened. "So, how long you in the city?"

"I live here," Ginger said, unprompted.

Jameison smiled and nodded. "How long you in the city?" He was studying me.

"I go back to LA after Christmas," I said.

"LA? What? You some kind of a reverse snowbird?" Jameison asked.

I laughed. "No, I came out for work," I said and felt like I had said too much.

"I'm here for work too," Jameison said. "I love the seasons, but this cold is for the birds," the actor said. "I thought I'd be here for a couple of months and then head back home, but the play I'm in is doing well."

"Really, well," Wild Bill Porter said with a smile.

Jameison looked at Porter and the manager smiled, awkwardly.

"I just don't like the cold," Jameison said.

"You telling me? I like New York, but man is it cold," I said with a shake of my head.

I couldn't get over being so close to Jamal Jameison. Jameison caught me staring at him, longingly.

"You got that whole Pretty Woman thing going on in your head? Huh? Don't you?" Jameison asked unexpectedly.

Jameison's question jarred me. I was a little surprised. I tried to recover. I knew the movie allusion and thought about it.

"I am not saying that doesn't happen," Jameison said after the food arrived. "I'm just saying that doesn't happen for us."

"What you mean?" I asked, confused.

"Well, I don't know a Cinderella story that begins with her being a stripper," I said.

I could not answer.

Thankfully, Ginger had an answer. "What about those bitches that came up?"

"Like who?" Jameison asked, curious.

"You know Cardi, and Trina and Eve were strippers?" Ginger said.

"I ain't judging," Jameison said. "But what I am saying is just because there are a couple of strippers who made a few songs, not every stripper is going to do that," Jameison said. He stopped. "Fuck it. I don't care. I'm just trying to have a good time on my birthday. I'm not trying to solve world issues tonight."

I did not respond.

"Yeah," said Flowers. "You get too in your head, Mall," Donovan Scott said.

The actor nodded. He ate and shucked off the concern as he concentrated on his meal.

"Did you look over the script I sent you?" Wild Bill Porter asked.

Jamal Jameison shook his head.

"I am supposed to remind you Mall, about the interview with New York Magazine tomorrow, " Flowers said, seeming to flip a switch to the day ahead.

"Tell Cody," Jameison said.

Ginger looked at me. I looked at her, seeing the mood change.

"What time is it?" Jameison asked.

"Nearly three," Cody Garland said.

"Cody, you go home," Jamal Jameison said with a smile. "Nothing else is going on tonight."

"You sure?" Cody Garland asked, uncertain.

Jameison looked at me and Ginger and the other girls. He nodded.

I looked at Ginger then to Donovan Scott. The promoter smiled, awkwardly. He shrugged.

"Think your night with Mall is over," he said, quietly.

With that Seneca, the bodyguard, talked to the second man and he climbed to his feet and walked to the table with Parisa, Bunny and Violet. The stranger spoke quietly with the three women.

"The fuck?" Ginger said, annoyed. "You ain't all that. You made some movies. Big deal. Just because you made some movies don't mean that you can fix us," she said. "And more importantly, we never said we needed fixing."

Seneca, the bodyguard, was suddenly beside the actor and seemed ready to tackle Ginger. Jameison shook his head and the bodyguard hesitated.

Flowers placed a hand on Ginger's arm. She twisted her arm free.

"Don't touch me," Ginger said in a hiss, climbing to her feet.

"Calm down, Ginger," I said. Bunny and Parisa climbed to their feet, protectively. Violet stopped eating her cheeseburger. She climbed to her feet and shook her head.

"Fuck that," Ginger said. "I don't care how many movies you made. We ain't broken and we don't need no fixing and more importantly you ain't doing me no favor talking to me," Ginger said.

"Fuck," I said. My night was over. My night with Jamal Jameison had come crashing down just like that.

Seneca stepped between Ginger and Jameison. The giant spread his arms to protect Jameison.

"Okay, you ladies have to leave," Seneca said.

I climbed to my feet as the diner employees and curious looked and videoed the ruckus. Ginger and the others moved toward the diner exit.

"Thanks for everything," I said to Jameison, who didn't even look up as we were ushered out of the diner by the two security guards.

Once, on the sidewalk, the two security guards stood at the door and watched as Ginger fumed and the others tried to figure out what to do.

"Fuck, Ginger," I said. I wanted to cry. Everything was going so well.

"Fuck them," Ginger said. She waved down a taxi and she and the others climbed in.

"You coming?" Parisa asked, confused.

"No," I said. I stood on the sidewalk and waved down a cab.

I gave the driver the name of the hotel. The cab headed back to the hotel. I rode in the back seat, dejected.

Chapter 6.

December 24.

One day 'til Christmas.

The next morning, I woke up around eleven o'clock. I climbed out of bed by noon. I showered, dressed, and went to get some food. As I climbed on the elevator headed for the lobby, I thought I would go to Times Square. I had not been there during the day and wanted to see all the glitz and glamour of the place.

In the lobby, I went to the concierge and asked for his recommendations for a good breakfast in Times Square. He produced a list and said that the top three choices were: Bibble & Sip, Toasties, and Times Square Diner and Grill.

"Now, I like all of them, but I find that the Diner and Grill is consistently my favorite for its simplicity and not trying to hustle you out," the concierge, an olive-skinned man with a trimmed and manicured beard said; dressed as though he was about to go to a wedding.

"Thank you," I said and headed to the front of the hotel. Central Park was on the other side of Frederick Douglas Avenue and just one hundred yards from the steps of the hotel. It looked idyllic. I hopped in a cab and rode to Times Square. At Times Square I was deposited near the epicenter of the icon location. I was dressed in my Dr. Marten 1460 boots, blue jeans, white sweater, and puff coat. On my head was my red Roots beanie. On my hands were my Roots matching mittens.

Times Square was a beehive of activity. People milled around going here and there. There were easily thousands of people just on the four blocks I could see. I could not imagine how many people had to be moving back and forth around Times Square at one time.

Not allowing the sheer numbers of the people to overwhelm me or the crowds to move me, I tried to head to the diner the concierge recommended. The walk was not that far. I walked past a half-dozen restaurants with the hope that the recommendation was accurate.

Finding the gaudy green Times Square Diner and Grill sign I entered the restaurant and found that it felt a little like a liquor store. There was a fully stocked bar and a liquor store in the diner as well as a section of the space dedicated to dining. I chuckled at the use of the space.

I was seated in the dining section and given a breakfast menu. Hiding behind my oversized sunglasses I ordered eggs with Turkey bacon, a fresh baked muffin, a fruit bowl, and orange juice. While I waited for my breakfast, I checked my messages.

Ginger had texted last night, after leaving the diner.

Sorry Goody. Things just got out of hand. I know you were starstruck. My bad.

A few minutes later I had another text from Ginger.

Call me tomorrow. Maybe we can have lunch or do something before you head back to LA.

I skimmed through the dozens of text messages looking for something. I did not find anything that interested me enough to open it. I stopped seeing Jesse's text message but refused to open it. I studied the ten words preview.

Hope you are well. Wanted to check on you over the holidays.

I ate my breakfast and thought about Jesse. If he hadn't been so clingy I might have texted back. Instead, as I finished my breakfast, I decided Los Angeles and Jesse and all boys trying to be men were a headache that I didn't need.

I was in New York City for just a few more days and I would go and explore Broadway. I was in the area. Before I left the diner, I picked up a Broadway guide and found that there were a dozen theaters in the immediate area.

I walked to Broadway and though it was not in the single digits, I felt I was doing okay. I was not freezing. The buildings blocked most of the wind and cold, I imagined.

I took a few pictures in front of theaters where famous plays were being performed. I had always wanted to see a musical performance but never found the time or motivation. So, I stopped in front of marquees and snapped pictures with me in front of them. Very touristy.

A familiar sight, while I was trying to avoid the cold of December, was the edifice of the Porn Mansion party. During the day it was a hotel. At night, well a few nights ago, it was so much more than I imagined. I had dipped my toe in the legitimate adult entertainment world. I was hoping that something would come from the trip to the east.

I walked just one block over and found the famous marquees of theaters that housed the performances of one of the longest running plays in New York. I had seen the movie -- or part of it -- and gotten bored trying to understand how no one knew there was a crazy man hiding in a theater. I guess that was the idea of musicals and theater. The more unlikely the more interesting and believable.

Just down the street was the marquee of the play Jamal was performing in. It was a limited run. It ended the second week of the new year. I approached and looked at the displays with Jamal and the other actors and actresses captured behind the glass on stage.

I stood at the theater and took a picture as I had done with the other theaters, but this picture after I took it made me a little uneasy. For the first time, I felt like a stalker.

I did not know what I wanted, but I did not want to be some creepy fan. I mean, I had met my crush. I had fantasized about Jamal Jameison sweeping me off my feet, like in the fairytales, but I knew that was crazy. Jamal had said it and now it made more sense. I had dreamed and made up a Pretty Woman fantasy where Jamal Jameison fell in love with me. I shook my head. That was stupid. He did not know me. I did not know him.

I was the Tongue Goddess. I was going to get back to LA and when I returned Porn Mansion was going to give me an audition. I did not need Jamal Jameison to save me. I was going to save myself.

I was going to pull myself out of the shit show that was my life of sucking and blowing and make something out of my talents. I did not care what it looked like to anyone else. I could not. It was my life. It was all I had. I was determined and not living in a fantasy.

I turned, to return to Times Square, and ran into Donovan Scott and Cody Garland.

"What are you doing here?" Donovan Scott asked, with a smile, dressed in a warm jacket, jeans, and boots.

"It's a free country, the last I looked," I said.

"Yeah, you're right, until they change that," Donovan Scott said with a small smile. "No. Seriously, what are you doing here? Looking for Jamal?"

I shook my head. "I was in the area and thought I would walk around the theater district," I said. "People do that when they visit New York," I said with a little smile.

Cody Garland, bored with Donovan and my conversation, walked to the stage entrance of the theater and entered.

"Well," Donovan Scott said, awkwardly. "It was definitely different last night with you and your friends."

I shrugged my shoulders in response.

Donovan nodded and walked to the stage entrance.

I walked away from the theater and headed to Rockefeller Center. According to the map it was only a few blocks from Broadway.

New York City was surprising because no matter the time of day there were always a large number of people walking on the streets. I read somewhere that most people in New York City did not drive because of the convenience of the subway and taxis. As I walked to Rockefeller Center, I recalled that there were nearly nine million people living in New York. I did not see all nine million, but I felt like I saw at least one million before reaching the iconic Rockefeller Center and the gigantic Christmas tree.

I entered the side of the Center with the two gigantic angels and below them the ice-skating rink. At the far end of the skating rink was the largest Christmas tree I had ever seen. It was fifty feet tall if not larger. The fresh pine smell permeated the air. The tree was just a magnificent full pine specimen. At the base of the tree, which was easily twenty feet across, was a golden angel sculpture. From my vantage point I could see that the Center was not one level but two. Beneath my feet was another floor of stores and offices all lit up and decorated for the holidays.

The whole Center looked like a postcard picture. I made my way around the Center clockwise heading toward the pine fresh smell of the giant Christmas tree. I window shopped and again was surprised that though it was cold it was not as cold as I had experienced previously.

When I reached the Christmas tree proper, I took an obligatory picture and headed back to the street I had come from to get a taxi back to my hotel.

Near the busy street I had the bad luck of running int Todd Dougherty. Dougherty was dressed in his black leather pants and well-worn boots. He was wearing an open winter jacket with a button front shirt, buttoned and an ugly green and red sweater. He almost looked normal that afternoon. When Dougherty saw me, he was with a woman that I assumed was his wife. She was a redhead with a pinched look and near her were two boys, not more than nine or ten. The two boys had the same pinched face resemblance to Dougherty and the woman.

He smiled recognizing me and nodded as I walked past.

"Happy holidays to you," Dougherty said, but I did not return the holiday wishes. Dougherty was pond scum that I had to wade through to get to the other side.

When I returned to the hotel, I called Ginger.

"You hungry girl?" Ginger asked, wearing a green cable knit sweater, her hair piled on top of her head somehow.

"I am," I said, with a smile.

"Okay, give me thirty and meet me at Melba's," Ginger said. "I'm leaving now."

I walked down to the concierge and asked him about Melba's.

"It is one of the best soul food restaurants in Manhattan," the concierge said with a smile. "It's a great place, at the northernmost end of Central Park, to get southern comfort food." He paused. "It's on the border of Harlem."

I looked at the concierge and smiled.

"Thanks," I said and headed to the exit. I caught a cab to the northernmost tip of Central Park. The ride took all of fifteen minutes from the hotel to Melba's restaurant. I climbed out of the taxi on Frederick Douglas Avenue and saw the burnt red awning and white letters that proclaimed the modest restaurant. Standing outside was Ginger, dressed in a knee-high suede boots, jeans, a three-quarter length puff coat with faux fur collar and hood. She was wearing the same green cable knit sweater. Her hair was hidden beneath a faux fur Cossack hat.

"What? No Parisa? Bunny? Or Violet?" I asked.

"Not today," Ginger said. "They were unavailable." Ginger smiled. "It is nearly Christmas."

I nodded.

Now, as we entered the small restaurant with polished wood floors and white walls we were met by a smiling woman.

"Welcome to Melba's," said high yellow woman with a loosely curled Afro and wearing a black and white polka dotted jacket and black dress. The greeter had a toothy grin, round cheeks, and big eyes.

"Hey," said Ginger. "Just us two," she added.

"Just you two," the greeter said with a smile. She looked to the wait staff, and one separated from the cashier and approached. The waiter was a thin, young man with a crown of black twisties. He was dressed in long-sleeved shirt and black trousers. On his feet were black basketball shoes. Around his waist was tied an apron.

"If you will follow Fisher, he'll take you to your table," the greeter said with a big smile.

Fisher smiled and turned on his heels and led us to an open table. I took in the interior of Melba's. It was quaint. It had a brick wall bar, with three columns of ceiling to bar mirrors. The interior of Melba's had a friendly but modern feeling with its white walls and black accents. The tables were black and so were the wooden chairs.

"Hope this will be fine," Fisher said, with a slight bow, directing us to the table. Fisher pulled out the chair for Ginger. Ginger smiled. She slowly sat down. Fisher gently pushed in her chair. The waiter stepped to my side of the table and pulled out my chair. He smiled. I sat and Fisher pushed in my chair slightly. Before he departed Fisher magically produced two menus for us and bowed and walked away to check on others.

"That was weird? Right?" Ginger said, once Fisher was out of earshot.

"Not that weird," I said. I tried to guesstimate Fisher's age.

"He seen your video?" Ginger asked.

"Probably," I said. "He looks like someone who might."

Ginger laughed.

When Fisher returned, he had two glasses of water. He placed them before us like we were royalty. He then took our orders.

It being the holidays Ginger and I ordered Chicken and Eggnog Waffles. Ginger had Mac 'N Cheese and Collard Greens. For my side I ordered Collard Greens and ASAP Yams.

"What would you like to drink?" Fisher asked.

"Is the bar open?" I asked.

Fisher looked back and saw that there was someone sitting at the bar. He turned back and smiled.

"Yes, it is," Fisher said, studying me.

"Okay," I said. "Can I have an Agave Kiss?"

Fisher frowned unfamiliar with the name of the drink. He smiled and nodded.

"I'll see if they can make that," Fisher said. "And for you, miss?"

"Can I have a Chocolate Martini?" Ginger asked when Fisher looked at her.

Fisher nodded and turned on his heels and walked away.

"This happen to you often?" Ginger asked.

"Not that often," I said.

I looked around the small restaurant and took in the dozen people sitting and eating. Ginger fished out her cellphone and checked a message.

"So, what you have planned for tomorrow?" Ginger asked.

"Not much," I said. "I figure I will camp out in my hotel room most of the day. I might go to Rockefeller Center. I went there earlier. It is beautiful." I paused. "I am just across from Central Park. I might do a walk around there." I shrugged my shoulders, unsure. "What are you doing?"

"Well, I have family here. So, I plan on seeing them and maybe having dinner with my sister," Ginger said. She looked at me sympathetically. "If you want you can come over my house and hang with my family."

"No," I said, raising my hands for emphasis. "I'm a big girl. I'll be fine."

Fisher returned with the drinks. He smiled as he sat my Agave Kiss in front of me. He expertly placed Ginger's Chocolate Martini in front of her.

"Enjoy," Fisher said, bowed, and disappeared.

We both looked at our drinks and smiled.

"Cheers," we both said and clinked our glasses together with a light chuckle. My Agave Kiss was as good as the first time I tried it at the hotel bar. I tried to think if I had ever had a drink as good as the Agave Kiss.

"This is good," Ginger said.

"Impressed," I said, looking to the bar and woman behind the bar. I raised my glass and smiled. Fisher, by the bar, smiled and nodded.

"So, you going to be okay on your own?" Ginger asked.

"I'm a big girl," I said.

"I know. I had to ask," Ginger said with a smile. "So, tell me what happened with you and the actor?"

"Nothing," I said. "You were there. He was cool and then he wasn't cool."

"Yeah," Ginger said. "Money warps your perspective, you ask me."

"I do have some news though," I said, cautiously.

"What?" Ginger asked.

"Porn Mansion wants to give me an audition," I said with a smile.

"An audition?" Ginger asked, cocking her head to the side.

"Yeah," I said.

"Congratulations," Ginger said.

Just then Fisher returned with our order. He placed the meal in front of us and bowed and disappeared.

Ginger lifted her drink.

"Well, girl, you on your way," Ginger said.

"Yeah," I said. "We'll see."

Ebony Goddess Erotic Adventures

Book Two
Written by T'Kendrae M. Ernest

Episode 1.

Miss Griffin's, the MILF, Favorite Things

My divorce was nearly five years ago. I hadn't been on a date in nearly a decade. It was twelve days before Christmas, and I decided I would give myself a present.

I slipped on my yellow panties and yellow laced bra. I grabbed a pair of comfortable flats. I slipped on my green holiday skirt and a white and yellow ruffle front blouse. I studied myself in the mirror. In the reflection was a caramel-skinned woman with long braided, shoulder length hair, arched eyebrows, brown eyes, round cheeks and two moles, one above my lip and one below my left eye. My hair was pulled back and away from my face. Though I was dangerously close to fifty I still looked good.

I climbed into my dark blue Mustang and drove to the mall looking for some gifts for my family. With twelve days until Christmas, I still had some shopping to do. I needed to get one last gift for my daughter Bridget and my two nieces, Jennifer and Dominique before mailing them off. They were the only ones in my family that I ever bought gifts for anyway. Bridget lived in Atlanta. My two nieces lived in DC with my brother Paul.

The local mall was crowded when I arrived and parked my car. There were dozens of people walking to their cars or heading to the mall. I scanned the faces of several men as I walked to the mall, trying to imagine kissing complete strangers. The idea was titillating. I smiled at a few men as I walked into the mall and the sea of faces.

Three gifts, I thought as I headed to Macy's. I liked Macy's because they seemed to have everything that I wanted in one store. I stopped at the Fragrance and Cosmetics department and perused the selection. Now, thinking of Bridget, I knew that she loved expensive perfume. I considered buying her a bottle of Black Opium. Then I noticed there was a bottle of Fenty available. I bought that knowing that it was hard to find.

One present down and two to go, I thought, as I paid for the distinct perfume.

I walked toward the exit and saw a couple of young men talking near the railing. Again, in my head, I fantasized about kissing one or both of them. I smiled and nodded to the two as I walked by.

I walked to the other end of the mall, looking for stores that would cater to a twelve- and fifteen-year-old. Jennifer was all into ClikClak and IndyVideo and trying to be an influencer. I figured I would go by Shop Smart and get her something to enhance her influencer dreams. For Dominique, who was on the cusp of being a teenager, I had no real idea.

At the familiar blue and gold price tag shaped sign and entrance I walked into Shop Smart. A greeter, dressed in a Shop Smart dark blue polo shirt smiled and studied me as I entered the store looking for the computer area. I turned right and on the other side of the entrance was Customer Service. Just past Customer Service was the Nerd Team area. To the left of the Nerd Team were all the computers and computer accessories.

While in Shop Smart I saw a man looking at me. I smiled. He smiled. Nothing came of my undirected flirtation. I bought Jennifer a halo light for her video blogging.

Leaving the mall with two of the three gifts I needed, I headed home. It felt good to feel men's eyes on me. I liked the harmlessness of flirtation. Yet, I wanted more.

I stopped at a light and a man in a black shiny car pulled up alongside me. I looked at him and smiled. It was innocent. He looked and looked away uninterested. I did not think I was everyone's cup of tea. So, though the unknown stranger did not give me my needed attention, I was not deterred.

I was feeling confident. Complete strangers looked at me longingly. All I had to do was stop and those longing looks could have become something tangible. Could have?

When I finally drove home, I opened my garage door and parked the Mustang. I climbed out of the car but did not close the garage. Instead, I looked out the garage and saw that my neighbor Cindy's son was visiting for the holidays. Jason Clark was a junior at a college in Boston. He was studying computers or engineering. Jason had a big brain. Cindy told me about Jason and his college experience anytime she had a chance.

"How you doing Miss Griffin?" Jason said, retrieving something from the trunk of his compact car.

I smiled and studied the boy that had become a man since my divorce.

"I'm good Jason," I said. "You tell your mom that I said: Hey."

"I will," Jason said and closed his car trunk, holding a duffel bag. He smiled and headed toward his house.

In a panic I took a few steps forward and waved to Jason to get his attention.

"Jason, if you aren't too busy and it's not any trouble," I said, from the garage. "Could I ask you to help me with something in my house?"

Jason stopped and turned at his name. He stood on the walkway to his house holding the duffel bag in his hand. He smiled and nodded, listening.

"Sure," Jason said. "Give me a minute to drop this off and I'll come right over."

"Okay," I said with a devilish grin.

I clicked the garage door opener and the paneled door slowly closed. I entered my house and feverishly tried to devise a plan. I wanted this to be a no-strings-attached kind of thing. I needed some relief. Jason wasn't going to be home all the time. Maybe I could jerk him off or he could play with me? The idea made me pause. I hadn't been touched, intimately, by a man in nearly half a decade.

I quickly ran to the kitchen and scanned the space for a problem Jason could fix. I deposited my two bags on the kitchen table. I scanned the kitchen for something to be broken. I didn't want to break something expensive.

I reached for the light bulb in one of the kitchen lights and unscrewed it, just enough so that it did not work. I flicked the light switch and made sure the light did not come on. I then scampered to my bathroom and did the same thing to one of the bathroom lights. That seemed pretty simple. I flicked on the light and the light fixture flickered in an almost strobing effect. The last light I unscrewed was in my bedroom.

While in the bedroom, I removed my panties. I unbuttoned my blouse and unhooked my bra. I decided I had to be ready and willing. I quickly straightened my ruffle front blouse and took a deep breath. No bra. No panties. I laughed as I deposited my bra and panties in the laundry basket as the front doorbell rang.

Walking without panties was interesting. It was not a drastic change but the one thing I noticed was the rub of fabric against my naked skin beneath my skirt. Now, I was big chested and walking without a bra was definitely something to get used to. My boobs seemed to have minds of their own. I took a deep breath and pressed my elbows against my sides and that seemed to contain my swaying tits a little better than before.

Thankfully, the front door was not very far. I took another deep breath and opened the door. There, in front of me, stood Jason Clark with his well-manicured hair style. He was six foot one inches tall, handsome, short-haired, with straight eyebrows, dark eyes, a foxlike nose that rested above a wide smile.

"Hi, Jason," I said, looking over my potential stress reliever. "Thank you for doing this," I beamed ushering him into the house.

"Sure," Jason said. He stepped into the house dressed in a T-shirt and blue jeans. On his feet were basketball sneakers. "No problem. I'm happy to help."

"Good," I said closing the front door.

"So, what seems to be the problem?" Jason asked, curious.

"Well, as you probably know I divorced my husband and there are just a few minor things that I need a little help with around the house," I said, wanting to laugh at the double entendres laced in the conversation that only I was aware of.

Jason nodded. He was tall, maybe six-inches taller than me. If I hugged him, I calculated, my face would hit just below his nipples.

"I understand," Jason said. He looked around the quiet and empty house. "So, what do you need me to fix?"

I paused. I wanted to just blurt out: Me. I wanted to lift my skirt and point to my untouched mound and say: This. I wanted to say a few words, but instead I pointed to the kitchen light.

"The light is out, and I can't figure out why," I lied.

Jason nodded. He looked around the kitchen and found the light switch. He clicked it on and off. True to my word, the kitchen light did not come on.

Jason walked to the light and felt the bulb. He twisted it and finding it was loose screwed it in tightly. He frowned. Jason shook his head.

"Seems that the bulb was not screwed in completely," Jason said and walked to the light switch and flicked the kitchen light on. The light illuminated the kitchen. I nodded. Jason smiled having solved a problem.

"That is so weird," I said with a coquettish smirk.

"No biggie," Jason said. "Things happen. Is there anything else?"

"Yeah, the same thing is happening in the bathroom," I said, pointing deeper into my home and closer to my bedroom.

We walked back to the bathroom. Jason flicked on the light switch. The light fixture above the sink was not one light but six. I knew that unscrewing one of the lights would effect all of the lights.

The light fixture flicked on and flittered. It was almost like a disco ball effect. I narrowed my eyes as did Jason. Jason turned the light on and off. The flickering continued.

He walked into the bathroom and examined the fixture. He touched the lights, one at a time. He unscrewed and screwed them back in methodically. He moved from the rear of the bathroom and slowly towards me. I watched him systematically check and tighten the light bulbs. The last light bulb he checked was loose.

"Ah," Jason said. "Here's the problem." He smiled.

I stood, leaning against the doorjamb, watching, with my elbows at my sides to direct my breasts toward Jason as he approached. I stood my ground as Jason stopped and smiled at finding the cause of the lighting problem.

Book Two of the Ebony Goddess Erotic Adventures Coming Soon